THE SHADOW
OVER CLEVELAND

Thirteen Lovecrafted* Tales

By Craig A. Webb

* Love-craft (luv'-kraft) *v.* **-crafted -crafting**

To create, embellish, or imitate in style, spirit, or

content the horror writer Howard Phillips Lovecraft.

-Love'-craft-ism *n.* **-Love'-craft-ist** or **-Love'-craft-er** *n.*

Burning River Productions
1601 Cook Ave.
Cleveland, OH 44109 - 5632

Copyright © 2015 Craig A. Webb
Cover Illustration, Ken Schworm www.kenschworm.com
Book layout, Sarah Sawaya, Sassafras Design Services
Editing, Tim Staveteig www.myliterarycoach.com
Author photograph, Ria Terranova-Webb

ISBN 978-0-9968861-1-6 (paperback)
ISBN 978-0-9968861-2-3 (ebook)

burningriver@msn.com

DEDICATIONS

My father, Robert Jay Webb
for scary stories told around the campfire

Special thanks to Sarah Willis, Laurie Kincer,
The Cuyahoga County Public Library, and
fellow members of its Writers' Workshops

Howard Phillips Lovecraft (1890-1937) was a reclusive, little-known writer of fictional horror stories. Descending from a family beset by madness and suffering from fragile physical and emotional health, Lovecraft struggled to earn a living from his writing. He died in abject poverty of malnutrition and intestinal cancer.

However, admiring fellow writers published his tales of horrific elder gods, forbidden lore, and evil madness set in his beloved New England posthumously, giving birth to a unique genre of literary horror. Thus the dark tortured genius of H. P. Lovecraft lives on—lurking in the shadows and inspiring these tales.

Contents

LAKE EFFECT
(Edgewater Park and Beyond)

He was a strange old bird, a bit comic and a little creepy, with his wide pirate smile and Vincent Price moustache. I had some idea what he wanted, but wasn't sure how I'd respond. Certainly it wouldn't hurt my chances in the department to play at being the professor's pet.

Standing in the ornate lobby of a Victorian-style apartment buildings across from Edgewater Park, I pushed the button beside his name on the engraved brass directory. He buzzed me right up.

"Craig," he said, upon opening the door, "how kind of you to accept my invitation. I'm sure you and I will have a wonderful time tonight."

"We'll see," I said, with a non-committal James Dean shrug. It was an impressive apartment, with lots of expensive-looking antiques and a good view of the lake. He wore about the same professional stuff he sported in class, minus the tie and tweed jacket. I stuck with my jeans, t-shirt, and sneakers. If he expected fancy dress-up, he wasn't getting it from me.

Dinner was still cooking so we had some time to kill. He poured me a glass of wine and asked if I wanted to get high. I was surprised, but didn't let it show. "Why not?" I said, sharing the joint he offered. Things got mellow after that. We talked a little politics. He was mildly interested in my anti-war protest adventures. Maybe getting clubbed and tear gassed by the police turned him on.

I helped set the table and we shared a decent meal. Probably expensive gourmet something-or-other, but what the hell did I know or care?

Afterward, we talked about my first year in the theatre department, the classes I'd taken, and the parts I'd played. He was planning to direct *Jesus Christ Superstar* after summer break and asked if I wanted to audition for the title role. A singing savior was not my forte, but maybe my long hair gave him ideas.

"Nah, you should give it to one of the real Bible-thumpers in the department," I said. "I'd rather do something with more red meat—like Caiaphas the high priest or Judas Iscariot."

He laughed. "Well, *that* would certainly enhance your reputation as our resident bad boy!"

"Right," I replied, "Everybody needs an angle in this business."

Outside, the summer sun was preparing for its nosedive into the western end of Lake Erie. If things were going to get slinky, it was time for him to put on some mood music and make his move. Instead, he suggested we watch the approaching sunset from the cliff edge. We finished off the joint and headed across Lake Avenue into the park.

It was a warm evening. A smattering of families and courting couples staked out ringside seats for the show. He picked a secluded spot and we sat down in the grass, waiting for our planet to rotate.

"It should be a good one," I said. "Just the right mixture of scattered clouds and jet-vapor trails to make it interesting."

"It would be even more interesting on this," he said, holding out a hand to me with two small squares of paper in his open palm. It was blotter acid; a brand I called *Jolly Rodger* because of the *Grateful Dead* skull printed on each square. Powerful stuff...whatever game he and I were playing; the stakes reached a whole new level. Dropping acid would make a long night of it. We wouldn't be touching back down until late tomorrow morning.

"How's that reputation of yours doing now?" he asked. I took one square of paper and purposefully swallowed it without chewing. He did the same.

"Holding steady," I said. "But yours is getting weirder by the minute."

Because we were both a little drunk and a lot stoned, it was difficult to pinpoint the exact moment our more transformational psychedelics kicked in. But, by the time the great burning eye of the sun extinguished itself under the boiling liquid horizon, I was pretty sure we achieved lift off. Before that, my professor wisely protected our vulnerable retinas by shifting attention to the origins of the lake.

"Imagine a mile-high wall of ice across the horizon," he said. "All slowly melting away into this immense glacial basin we call Lake Erie. Picture a vast inland ocean, with its shoreline way further south beyond the borders of Cleveland, and its current running west toward the Mississippi instead of east over Niagara Falls."

"Was anyone here to see that?" I wondered. "I mean cavemen or Indians or someone?"

"Nothing human. Homo sapiens came much later over the land bridge from Asia. But things arriving frozen inside that glacial tsunami can still be found in our lake today.

"Are you talking about dirt and rocks, or shit dissolved in the water, like salt and minerals?"

"I'm talking about things living in the arctic regions eons ago, my boy, when they were still quite temperate. Things that were flash frozen, so to speak, when Earth's magnetic poles shifted."

I tried to comprehend what those things might be. The descending darkness sent all other sunset enthusiasts scurrying back to their cars and pickups. The gear growls and engine snarling of their mass exit filled the night air. Their head and taillights darted here and there in a frenzy of glaring advances and blood-red retreats.

"What's their hurry?" I wondered.

"Fear," my companion said, "of the dark...and each other. There's no telling, 'what evil lurks in the hearts of men,' and so on. We are a dangerous breed."

He and I found ourselves alone now, at the southern-most reach of a much-diminished inland sea. Our heightened perceptions craved the whisperings of the water. The ancient tales told only by waves against shoreline. For our ravenous eyes, the dance of moonlight upon liquid promised an optic feast. Later on the distant endless boundary of air and water would disappear completely, adding to the potency of our vision. But for this, we had to get closer.

We climbed down the wooded slope to a hidden section of shoreline below the parking areas. Standing on the edge of that vast rippling darkness, we experienced the life force of the entity we call Erie. Now possessed of keener senses, we used them; heard water, held stone, saw moonlight, and breathed in deeply the strong aromas of damp air and rotting fish.

"Do these pungent remains bother you?" he asked.

"A little," I confessed.

"Death is an essential part of this life experience, my young friend. Do you suppose our decaying flesh—laying on this shoreline or elsewhere, instead of being embalmed, stuffed into coffins, and buried six feet under—would smell any better?"

"Probably not, but at least the police would cart us away so nobody else would need to smell it."

We shuffled along the water's edge over wave-piled mounds of smooth rounded pebbles the color of roasted coffee beans. Here and there the rising moonlight glistened off lustrous jewels of commercial color. Nuggets of cola clear, uncola green, and ale amber were seeded generously. Reds and blues were rare, their origins more mysterious. Transformed by the interplay of sand and waves, these fairy treasures would change into mere scratched glass if we stole them from Erie's liquid embrace. With our heightened senses overloaded, we felt the need to increase our receptive zones. We decided to carry our shoes.

Resting on the limestone blocks of the break wall, feet dangling in the dark water, we exchanged our experiences of this northern edge of our city.

"Sometimes," he said, "This is a battleground. These fortresses of broken stone are all that stand between Cleveland and the ferocity of the angry lake. But tonight, there's a truce. For our benefit, they make music together, with liquid sound waves approaching from the opposite shore."

"Last November, I brought the whole cast of my Shakespeare production out here," I said. "In the middle of a thunderstorm. I made them shout their lines into the teeth of the wind and waves to get a feel for medieval Scotland. I even asked the guy playing Macbeth to murder my cat, for a better grasp on his character."

We both broke out in hysterical laughter at the stark impropriety of that request. Suddenly police cruiser headlights swept along the top of the break wall. They were making their protective rounds looking for after-hours partiers. Our laughter must have drawn them in our direction. Hiding in a dark crevasse between huge stone blocks, we managed to elude misdemeanor trespassing, while chemical criminality raced through our bloodstreams pumped by the adrenaline of possible discovery.

"So did he kill your cat?" he whispered.

"Hell no, he wimped out. He said I was seriously crazy to even suggest it." A long pause followed. I could feel his hot breath close upon the back of my neck as we huddled together in the moist darkness.

"Well," he asked. "Do you think you're crazy?"

"Sometimes," I admitted.

"Are you crazy enough for a midnight swim?"

There it was, the opening move of the come-on I expected after dinner. Up in his apartment, I would have laughed him off, smug in my ability to both attract his desire and thwart it. But now, we shared an alternative reality. Disrupting the flow of our adventure would negate all that had gone before and any unknown discoveries yet to come.

The very essence of an epic acid trip or a good improvisation was surrendering to the affirmative. Saying yes, to every new emotion and experience. Exuberantly accepting new possibilities and even impossibilities as they presented themselves.

"The water is filthy," I warned.

"And we've forgotten our bathing suits," he observed.

"And there's no lifeguard," I added.

"Absolutely anything could happen," he teased.

"That settles it," I said. Our clothing came off. My inhibitions fell away almost as easily.

Moving out into the warm water, the night air transmitted the chill of deep space while the liquid retained thermal energy from our aging star. It was a womb stretching as far as we could see and still further, back into forgotten time and unknown origins.

Gently flowing, we luxuriated in the smooth movement of our bodies weightless in a fluid world. Eyes level with the continuous plane of surface: we were just a ripple of moonlight away from floating up into the starry above, or sinking down into the inky depths. It was an ancient evolutionary choice we found tempting.

Erie did tempt us. She beaconed us out ever farther, offering to end this life journey and begin another. I might have gone—in a sense I wanted to go. Some other night the lake might grasp hold of us, might drag us out and under, might dash us against her stony boundaries until we were torn to pieces—but not tonight.

This night Erie entertained her lovers. If any were lost, they surrendered to the seduction of her embrace, not the violence of her will. So we floated. Swam a ballet. Dove under to the airless heart of her mysteries and surfaced again to her ceiling of moon and stars.

We gazed at Cleveland's illuminated carnival shoreline like alien fish-men up from the deep. Downtown and the towers of the Gold Coast competed for our amazement, as they tossed their speeding steel vehicles back and forth on the west shoreway.

Somehow, the lighted skyscrapers, bridges, and freeways made me think of roller coasters, Ferris wheels, and rocket-ship rides. It was as if the Euclid Beach Amusement Park of my youth hadn't died. Instead it spread itself out all along the lakefront, dazzling me into childhood again.

Eventually I got cold. It could have taken minutes, but it felt like hours and hours. Coming back ashore was a kind of rebirth. We didn't rush to cover ourselves, standing together for some long sweet moments, to savor our savage nakedness on the shores of civilization.

"See this chaos created by so-called humanity," my professor hissed. "This madness built by the inferior descendants of the mammalian rat-race, who overran this planet while their betters lay in frozen slumber. Their egg-devouring ancestors so decimated the elder races they must now cohabitate and interbreed with their enemies to survive."

"Look who's seriously crazy now," I said, turning away from him to walk back to where we hid our clothing.

"Wait, my young friend," he pleaded, grabbing hold of my arm. "There's something more I need to share with you."

"I know what you need," I said. "I knew when I agreed to come over. Let's go back to your apartment, where we can shower and be more comfortable."

"You know nothing!" he growled. "Your tiny egotistical mind cannot conceive of what I'm offering—of what awaits you, right here on this beach. Tonight you have the opportunity to become part of something far greater than yourself."

As he forcibly restrained me, spouting strange gibberish of sunken cities and ancient destiny, I looked past his alarming intensity toward the dark lake. Unearthly lights played below its surface as luminous forms approached the shoreline from far below.

"This is our ancient heritage," he insisted. "The future of our city, the means to transform our limited species!"

His words and the powerful drug we consumed, spawned strange ideas and desires in my mind, sapping my will to resist.

"Look for yourself! The warm night, the calm lake, and a full moon," he explained. "Triggers this fertile surfacing of willing amphibious paramours."

As he drew me back into the dark Lake, the ripening Vaarg maidens arose gracefully from its waters. Their naked pale-green luminescence, moon-like eyes, and scaly tresses sparkled under veils of water droplets, exciting me in unspeakable ways. For this was mating season, and the professor and I were needed to share our inferior but necessary seed.

SCREAMER

(The Union—Aetna Neighborhood)

In an isolated ethnic neighborhood south of Union Avenue, squats a gray, two-unit, wooden house that is old, but well kept. The house is on a backstreet and should be nearly indistinguishable from all the other working-class doubles crammed in around it. Yet every man, woman, and child in the neighborhood is aware of this house and has ideas about what goes on inside.

The enclave is small and insular—protected and imprisoned within desolate ramparts of factories, train tracks, and freeways. At the center of the neighborhood stands the aging edifice of St. Lawrence Church. Its bells toll away the hours of all who dwell there. The shadow of its bell tower comes to rest on the gray house every evening long before sunset, casting darkness upon this dwelling in advance of night itself.

I moved into the neighborhood last fall, an outsider drawn in by the offer of a free apartment with utilities in exchange for maintaining the property. Having just dropped out of Cleveland State University for lack of money, this seemed like a good deal. At first, I was too busy catching up with daytime repairs to notice anything. Not until the middle of October, when I finally moved in and began to hunker down for that long northern Ohio winter, did I become aware of her.

She lived right next door in the gray house. Her apartment perched on the second floor like mine. About fourteen feet of air and the dirty glass of two old windows separated us. Once she had my attention, I could hear her loud and clear.

In the inner city neighborhoods of Cleveland loud cars, emergency sirens, and domestic quarrels are the background noise of life. You learn to ignore them. But she was beyond ignoring. She would scream—I mean really cut loose with a shrill rasping voice. She would wail, moan, and grunt like a wrestler. Then she would begin to rant and rave, to berate, plead, and demand. After that, when she was completely warmed up, she would begin the torrential stream of profanities. Her curses scorched my ears. They gushed from her like water from a fire hose.

I'm no boy scout. I've let a few choice cuss words fly from time to time—but I never heard anything like this. I think only half of it was genuine English. She cussed in languages I couldn't come close to identifying. Maybe she made up her own language—spoke in tongues or something. I felt I should be taking notes, in case somebody royally pissed me off and I righteously wanted to come down on them.

At first, whenever I heard her, I was overcome with pity for the unknown target of her abuse. I pictured some poor little guy too old or ill to fight back—because I never heard any reply to her onslaughts. Maybe he was deaf and dumb. Being stone cold deaf would be a blessing under those circumstances—unless you could read lips.

Naturally I became curious. My landlord, who lived below me, never said a word about her. I wouldn't have either—if I were trying to coax some kid to move in. The talkative retiree on the other side of the gray house never mentioned her, although he jabbered all day about any other topic under the sun. I figured she must be a sore subject in the neighborhood—so I didn't rock the boat. Not until early November did I get any real information.

One Saturday night, as my landlord and I struggled with an emergency water heater replacement in the basement, she started in. At first he kept working like nothing was happening and so did I. Then she got going big time. The screams, growls, and threats became so intense and powerful no one could block them out. They absolutely compelled us to stop and listen.

When she subsided, my landlord let out a painful laugh and sighed, "Wow, she let all hell break loose tonight." I jumped at this opening.

"Yeah, she really lets him have it, doesn't she?" I said, shaking my head in pity. "Poor old son-of-a-bitch."

He stared back at me in puzzled shock. "Don't you know about her?" he asked. "No, of course not. Why should you? I forgot you're not a neighborhood kid. I should have warned you." I felt an unpleasant sensation run up my spine. "That's the worst thing about it. Nobody's up there with her—she lives alone."

Huddled in the basement, he told me all he knew about the old lady he called "the Screamer." My landlord purchased the property ten years ago, but she had lived upstairs next door as long as anyone could remember. Nobody ever visited her but the local priest. She never went out except to occasionally wander in circles around her back yard on sunny days. On those occasions, he said she appeared to be a normal heavy-set, old woman. "Not a local," he assured me. "I think she came from West Virginia somewhere."

An elderly ethnic woman who spoke little English lived downstairs in the gray house and seemed to take care of the Screamer in an almost motherly way—although nobody believed them to be related. The ethnic woman and her two grown sons handled all the shopping, maintenance, and yard work for the house and attended Mass together with clockwork regularity.

My landlord considered her mentally disturbed and her tirades directed at imaginary tormentors. Her fits did not occur every night and only occasionally reached great intensity and duration. "I think it's her time of month—you know," he theorized. "Some women get crazy like that."

Given her supposed age I doubted his explanation, but what did I know about geriatric PMS? These new clues explained a lot of things. At least I no longer had to feel sorry for a disabled spouse. My empathy shifted in her direction. I wondered if she'd ever seen a psychiatrist. I guessed the neighborhood too old school for such intervention. They simply left her alone, providing basic charity.

Later, I had conversations with her nearest neighbors who gave me the same story except for the timing. One blamed phases of the moon, like she turned into a werewolf or some shit. Another proposed Cleveland's bizarre weather and changing seasons as the random trigger. The general consensus was madness, but the elderly ethnics who tottered warily past the gray house on their way to the church claimed a ghost or devil inhabited the house itself.

The ghost part hit a sensitive cord with me, because my own apartment became none too quiet after dark. Lying in bed, I swore a dinner party of poltergeists held court in my kitchen. There were footfalls, doors opening, dishes rattling, water running—you name it. During the first month, I must have averaged at least two trips a night around the apartment and even downstairs into the basement looking for prowlers.

I never found anybody. I finally matched certain sounds to various plausible explanations based on my shaky knowledge of foundation settling, rodent activities, and ancient plumbing. I stopped thinking about the rest. After the novelty wore off, sometimes I lay awake listening on purpose. I tried to guess what my phantom guests fixed for dinner. But most of the time, I concentrated on overhearing who the Screamer thought she confronted and why.

I got nowhere with that. Although most of her words seemed decipherable, I found their aggregate meaning unknowable. It wasn't babble, but not coherent speech either. Before, I had tried to insert imagined rebuttals from an unheard husband. Now that I knew no husband existed, her silences became as cryptic as her tirades.

Then you had to consider the intensity. I had never heard a woman speak in this way. I had never heard these sounds come from a human mouth. She defined, in horrifying detail, my concept of the verb *to rave*. That brings me to the other sounds—the non-verbal din of madness. From what I heard, objects must have been thrown, smashed, and slammed. Chairs dribbled like basketballs, glass broke, fabrics tore, and things—extremely heavy things—went bump in the night.

Many times I would try to see into her apartment from my windows. I'd turn off my lights and try to make sense of the jumbled shadows playing across her shades. She always kept her blinds drawn down tight and would not allow even the slightest peep at the real performance inside.

My curiosity made me approach the elderly ethnic lady who lived below her one morning as she passed on the sidewalk. She proved as forthcoming as a stone. She knew so little English I was reduced to idiot pantomime in the effort to broach my subject. She simply uttered "no" to any question I attempted to ask. My efforts at acting things out made her back away warily.

When I pointed to myself and then up at the Screamer's apartment, her eyes grew wide as she seemed to catch some meaning. She shook her head slowly in horrified negation. Crossing herself defensively, she pushed past me and hurried in the direction of the church.

I began to ask about the madwoman's situation around the neighborhood, in grocery stores and at the corner bar. Women always shook their heads, drawing their coats in closer around themselves as if sheltering from a cold draft, and expressing heart-felt pity. Men started in on the subject with a howling laugh, followed by heartless grotesque impressions of the rants the Screamer made famous, and ending with the universal verdict of "she's fucking nuts." Then they would say no more about her.

I found myself going outside and circling the gray house at night during her attacks. Folks tended to lock up early in that neighborhood, so I became the only pedestrian lurking outside after dark. Occasionally a passing car would capture me in its headlights, causing me to feel implicated in some crime.

That's how I discovered the game. Holding a generally pessimistic view of humanity, I should have known someone would find a use for this old woman's misery. I learned a certain element of mean-spirited local youth found her entertaining.

They taunted her. Non-verbally and anonymously, they would do things to trigger or intensify her fits. Their favorite technique involved the loud nocturnal mutilation of her garbage cans.

I thought I discovered a source of her madness or at least its timing, but I was too optimistic. These boys occasionally bothered her from outside. Her real tormentors ravaged her from within.

I grew reckless. I contacted the local police about the boys. They were superficially sympathetic, but probably didn't give a damn about that neighborhood. Real murder and mayhem went on all around us in the ghetto neighborhoods 24/7. "Kids kicking cans" didn't rate a single drive-by from even one squad car. I defaulted to the only other authority I could imagine—the parish priest.

Old Father Zupancic was understanding—considering I'm not a local or even Catholic. "I am knowing this woman very well," he said, fingering his rosary compulsively. "I have greatest sympathy for her condition. I pray God gives to her the strength to endure." He praised the ethnic woman living under her and the woman's two sons for their selfless devotion, commending the neighbors also for their Christian understanding and forbearance. Then, he waxed poetic.

"Each must struggle against sin in our hearts and evil surrounding us," he whispered, as if someone other than me listened inside that empty cavernous relic of a sanctuary. "Give battle every night to protect righteous life," he pleaded, grasping onto my arm and shaking the small crucifix dangling from his beads in my face. "Only shield of faith saves us—this cross she carries alone!" I kept waiting for him to pass the collection plate.

The more he talked, the more I got the impression he saw her as some sort of martyr. How convenient. Ignore the sick woman—because God had need of her. I could not swallow any more.

"Look father, all this holy stuff is fine. I know what you're talking about. I used to go to church as a kid," I said, as rationally as possible. "But this woman needs real help. She needs to see a psychiatrist—she may even need to be committed. At least, we should get her to a social worker."

His demeanor changed completely. He grew hostile and accused me of godless meddling. I tried to back pedal, but the damage had been done. He pushed me out the church doors with a warning.

"Leave this woman!" he yelled, shaking with almost uncontrollable emotion. "Leave this place—I am warning to you! The devil find you—if you stay!"

His warning didn't work. The more self-righteous I became about my concern for this poor woman, the more I ignored my overpowering curiosity to see her in action. In the end, I almost manifested what happened by shear willpower.

Working in the garage one night on my rusty pickup, the Screamer began her familiar raving. She growled and cursed at a feverish pitch until I heard the sound of breaking glass. After that, she seemed to sputter out, and I returned my attention to replacing a leaky radiator hose. Then the local delinquents showed up. Sensing a rising curtain, I shut off my work light to conceal my attendance at the performance.

The first assault on the cans was modest. Just a few kicks and some spilled contents on the driveway. A burst of profanity erupted from the Screamer's apartment and the boys scattered. I saw the light at the top of her private stairs click on through the window on her back door. The blood in my temples started to pound in anticipation. I hoped to see the Screamer in action for the first time.

A heavy shadow descended the stairs. The light spilled out around her considerable bulk. She opened the door at the bottom of the stairs and peered out with a twisted hateful expression. I could see sweat dripping off her ruddy swollen face, although it was a chilly night. She muttered a few choice expletives at the darkness and shook her pudgy fist at the spilled garbage, then turned back inside abruptly. Her shadow retreated back up the stairs along with her horrible mutterings, but the stair light stayed on, and the door stood partially open.

I remained transfixed. Probably, this would have been enough for one night had I not witnessed what followed. The local bad boys returned to the scene of their crime en masse. Their second attack on her cans had such ferocity it tore the fabric of the night like the sound of a fatal auto crash. Upstairs, the Screamer exploded with mad raving and began to throw things around. I expected a chair to come through a window at any moment.

The boys responded by redoubling their efforts on the cans. The Screamer's voice split the night in rage, but the boys topped her immediately in galvanized carnage. Words failed her, and she began withering the treetops with snarling animal fury.

I'd had enough. Definitely someone was in pain upstairs. One flash of my work light and an appropriately husky shout scattered the boys instantly. Nevertheless, I advanced to the battered cans in a show of false bravado.

The Screamer hit her all-time high upstairs. Just as I wondered how anyone could scream like that and not be seriously injured, her tone abruptly changed into one of physical pain. The lighted stairway and unlocked door beckoned. Human compassion and raw curiosity pulled me forward. I'll never know which dragged me over the doorstep.

Inside the stairwell I felt dizzy and hot. My eyes began to water, going in and out of focus. I almost lost my balance, but instead of crashing to the floor, I felt about to fall up her staircase.

Above me I could hear the Screamer's voice crack. Her breath came in short painful gasps. Thinking heart attack or stroke, I heard the unmistakable sounds of a final throaty gurgling, and found myself at the top of the stairs.

I was sucked down a long dark hallway, seemingly so distorted and narrow my shoulders knocked countless crucifixes and pictures of the Virgin Mary from the walls as I passed. Somehow the length of that hallway appeared impossible for the outside dimensions of the house. A lighted room waited far ahead. No way in this world did I want to enter that room, but I discovered myself on its threshold anyway.

I saw a huge kitchen, all gleaming with ethnic attention to spotlessness. Everything appeared white and shiny. Every surface reflected like a spotlight in my eyes. In the center of an immense expanse of tiled floor, the old woman lay struggling feebly against a huge dark figure overpowering her. The shock of that sight overwhelmed comprehension. My eyes refused to focus properly. As I watched, the shape and size of her assailant flickered and changed. First I beheld a savage grinning man, then a bear, a goat, a snake, and back to a man again.

I stood paralyzed in the doorway until the woman saw me and thrust her hand out in my direction for help. The room seemed to tilt radically toward her as I teetered at its edge. I grabbed the door-frame, desperately trying to not fall into their arena, but a powerful onrushing wind from the hallway blew me helplessly into the out-stretched grasp of the gigantic dark figure.

I yelled for help. I hollered so loud the whole neighborhood must have heard me. I bellowed shamelessly like a terrified ox attacked by an army of butchers. His grasp crushed me like iron clamps. His touch burned my flesh like a red-hot stovepipe. His horrible, leering, scaly face hovered just inches from my own, and I *screamed!*

Then we were in an empty ordinary-sized kitchen. Just the old woman splayed out on the floor, with me standing in a ludicrous pose over her body. She wept. I stepped back to get my bearings. She grabbed me by the ankle and started to kiss my shoe. Torrents of tearful thanks poured from her upturned face.

I pulled away from her joyous expressions of gratitude and ran down the short hallway, stepping over one crucifix and a single broken picture of Mary. I flew down the stairway, jumped the overturned trashcans, and fled back into my apartment, slamming the door behind me.

She stopped screaming after that and moved away before Christmas. Nobody knows where she went. My neighbors regard me strangely on the street. I hide from them all day with my blinds drawn down tight. The landlord never asks me to help him anymore. Nobody talks to me except Father Zupancic, who comes to chat and bring me food prepared by kindly ethnic women in the neighborhood. They think I'm sick and in need of their charity.

I sleep during the day now and stand guard all night. Last night I caught the creature poking his dark scaly head out from behind my refrigerator. I cursed him at the top of my lungs and threw a shoe. He vanished, but I know he will be back.

OBSESSION
(The Main Public Library—Downtown)

Yolanda Scruggs trudged down Superior Avenue through yet another chilly Cleveland morning. The weather, the early hour, and the push-and-shove of those regarding her as mere obstruction—did not bother her. She was headed home to the grand stone edifice offering her refuge, the one place she felt she belonged. Not that she actually stayed there.

She stayed up on Cedar Road, in a sad double sliding toward decrepitude at a steady pace. But she didn't live there. You couldn't call that pitiful existence a life. She lived, worked, and found home in two places: the granite temple of knowledge known as the Main Library Building, and inside her solitary mind.

"Good mornin', Miss Scruggs," the elderly security guard said with a respectful nod, as she pushed through the revolving brass doors worn smooth and shiny by the touch of many hands.

"Hey, George," she replied. "How you be doin' today?"

"Old as dirt, but gettin' by," he joked. "How bout you, young lady?"

"I'm all right, now," she said with a smile, removing the old scarf and coat that covered her drab clothing and close-cropped hair. "I'm ready for another day in paradise."

Everyone who worked at the Main Library took this habitual comment as wry satire. Some chuckled, saying "Ah huh…if only!" But it wasn't a joke to Yolanda.

She passed the checkout desks, the glowing computer screens replacing her beloved card catalogs, ignored the elevators, and started up the massive marble stairs. She passed the stern white faces of former directors displayed on the landings between floors. Strange names, such as Luther Melville Oviatt and Irad L. Beardsley made her wonder what sort of odd folk had come before her, up these winding stairs, and down these silent stony halls.

On ascending to the third floor, Yolanda paused a moment before the marble portal of the John Griswold White Special Collections. "Ol' Gris" must have been the oddest of the bunch. A nineteenth century multi-millionaire so obsessed with the game of chess, he issued orders worldwide to buy up every conceivable publication ever written about or referencing the game...no matter the rarity or price.

Amassing the world's largest chess library might have been merely excessive, except for the fateful "or referencing" directive. Could he possibly have envisioned the bizarre ramifications of that? The chance metaphoric connections leading down so many obscure pathways into Folklore, Orientalia, and Demonology? Yolanda wondered if he was surprised, appalled, or delighted by all of that?

Unlocking the first set of ornate wrought-iron gates, she decided to table that inquiry for further investigation. Perhaps she would write an article on the subject for the *Journal of Library Science*. Walking the length of the exhibit corridor, gliding her ink-stained fingers over the many antique iron and glass display tables, she instead entertained her most cherished fantasy.

She dreamed of an award-winning novel that would someday be her own marvelous creation. A literary masterpiece containing details as intricate as Victorian architectural drawings, imagery as vivid as the jewel-like illustrations of the *Rubaiyat of Omar Khayyam*, characters as compelling as those in Arthurian legend, and plots as twisted and deep as the forbidden grimoire of Olaus Wormius. All these rich sources lay at her fingertips in the Collections, waiting to be absorbed and reimagined by her, for the unenlightened reader.

At the second set of gates she quelled these reveries. Through this last portal, she could see her beloved post at the Special Collections desk, and beyond, the breathtaking expanse of tall windows framing the green copper roofs of Cleveland's public buildings, the yellow-orange dawn, and the dark, rolling mystery of Lake Erie.

Yolanda cherished this moment. Unlocking the gates to her literary kingdom provided her indescribable joy, which explained why she arrived early, trying to ensure the moment wasn't spoiled by the intrusion of her coworkers. She had struggled long and hard to arrive here, enduring years of constant distraction in the busy periodical and popular departments. She even survived hated exile to the new "interactive" Louis Stokes Wing. There the primary attractions of CDs and DVDs, beloved by library patrons who despised actual reading, and the Internet computer banks foretold the inevitable extinction of the printed words she worshiped.

"Yo—Landa!" brayed her worst tormentor. "Are you gonna open that cell block or what?" She refused to say anything, knowing response was tantamount to encouragement for Tony. "What's up with you, Book Baby?" he asked. "Has Old Gris got your tongue?"

"I wish Ol' Gris would get your tongue," she mumbled, unlocking the gate as Tony elbowed past her. "Then I could get some work done in here."

"That old ghost has already got me," claimed the young preening fool, plopping into her chair and resting his shoes on the desk. "Why else would I be locked up in here with your sorry ass? I am cursed Book Baby, and that is a fact."

"You are being disciplined," corrected Dr. Gray, overhearing his complaint as she entered. "Yolanda and I are the ones being cursed... with your annoying company."

"That's cold, Doctor G.," Tony whined. "Like the black man said, after a couple dozen white cops beat his brains out, 'can't we all just get along?'"

"Of course, we can," she responded. "Why don't you 'get along' to the west storeroom and unpack the boxes from our offsite vault? We have a major exhibit happening this month and everything must be ready." Tony swung his feet off the desk, stood up, bowed sarcastically, and moved toward the storeroom.

"No use of box cutters, please!" Dr. Gray called after him. "Those books are worth more than you are."

"Just about anything would be," Yolanda added.

"That attitude is not helpful, Miss Scruggs," said their attractive, stylish supervisor. "Young Mr. Lucarelli will be transferred back to the Lewis Stokes Wing soon enough, and you'll have your peace and quiet back. He hasn't made any improper advances toward you has he?"

"No, Shelly. I mean...no, Doctor Gray."

"Good. Let me know if he does. He's on probation for excessive fraternization with the library's female clientele. If he lays a finger on either of us, I'll have him fired."

"I don't think we're Tony's type," Yolanda said.

"Oh," Shelly reacted, compulsively adjusting her fashionable business attire. "Uhmm...why not exactly?"

"Because we both have brains."

o———o

Later that day, as Yolanda worked on a rewrite for the exhibit of a clockwork automaton that famously defeated Napoleon at chess, Dr. Gray and Tony reappeared from the storeroom. They'd disappeared for hours, but only missed two elderly scholars looking for a German language libretto of the *Tales of Hoffmann*.

"I'm off to the main office," announced Shelly, hurrying by

straightening her silk scarf and jacket. "I should be back after lunch."

"Yeah, and I'm gonna go take a leak," claimed Tony, trailing her like a trained poodle. "Hold down the fort, Book Baby. I'll be back...you know, when I'm done." Yolanda never expected any real help from either of them. She smiled pleasantly as they exited and breathed easier in their absence.

After Yolanda settled back to work, an uneasy stillness took hold in the room. She sensed this change and prepared for what usually followed. Her neck and shoulders tensed slightly as the temperature around the desk area dropped, despite the late morning sunlight that should have warmed the room. A familiar cloud of dust motes floated expectantly in the sunbeams at the far left edge of her perception.

"Don't be botherin' me, Gris," she warned the taut emptiness around her. "I'm busy. You go spook Tony in the lavatory. Make him pee on his shoes."

A sudden noise emanated from the stacks up on the mezzanine level. The dust motes floated upward and drifted off down a mezzanine aisle just left of the solid area above the entrance. Another faint noise reached her ears. It sounded like a heavy reference book being carefully pulled from its shelf. *Perhaps Ol' Gris is onto something*, she thought. *We could have a climber.*

Access was strictly forbidden for anyone but staff on the mezzanine level. Consequently, their most rare and precious volumes resided up there. Occasionally someone tried to sneak up and wander around. Precious editions had disappeared. Her only visitors that day had been the elderly Germans, both of whom seemed too frail to totter up the stairs. But, they could have been decoys. An accomplice could have entered unseen as she helped them, while Tony and Dr. Gray busied themselves monkeying around in the storeroom. She'd have to check.

Unlocking the metal chain baring access to the stairwell, she climbed the narrow stairs. The air up here carried the scent of dust and disintegrating paper. *Musty* it was generally called, but there was something more to it in the Special Collections. She wondered if ideas, truly ancient ideas, had a certain aroma to them...*an odor of obscurity.*

Yolanda topped the stairs and moved out onto the balcony running outside the rows of shelves burrowing back toward the rear wall away from the light. Her own footprints remained faintly visible in the fine dust layer on the balcony floor. Nobody else had been up here. She could see that. Yet, when she peered down the aisle favored by the dust motes, sure enough, a thick oxblood-colored book appeared partially drawn out of line with the other volumes.

Oh bother, she thought. *Ol' Gris wants me to read this.* As she moved down the aisle, a strange sensation took hold of her. No matter how many steps she took down the row of shelves the book got no closer. Looking back toward the balcony, she knew she was as far down the aisle as she should be able to go, given all aisles measured less than twenty feet deep. But, when she turned to look toward the back wall, the aisle appeared to extend another and another and another twenty feet inward.

She stopped, closed her eyes, and rested her forehead against a shelf. She knew this could not be happening. She bit down hard on one ink-stained finger expecting to awaken at her desk. Instead she drew blood, and the pain of her bite confirmed she might be marooned in this haunted aisle as surely as Robinson Crusoe on his desert island.

She lowered her bleeding hand still unwilling to open her eyes, when she somehow touched upon the half withdrawn book. Amazingly she had found the book—or the book had found her—despite her untrustworthy perception. She tried to grasp it, but the elusive volume snapped back out of her grip into line with the other books like someone had snatched it from the other side of the bookshelf. Strangely, no "other" side to this shelf existed, because this section of bookshelves backed up onto the solid masonry above the Collections entrance.

How could there be another side? she thought. She knew the exhibit corridor had a high vaulted ceiling which ended in the second iron gates and the outer wall of the Collections room. Visitors passed through a tunnel-like portal, and found themselves facing the Collections desk. If I they turned around, they saw aisles of shelves to the left and right, repeated on the mezzanine level above...except for the solid center section above the portal, dominated by an ornate marble decoration.

Why hadn't she realized this before? There could be a space up there—possibly ten by twenty feet, depending on the thickness of the walls. But, how did anyone get inside and what...or who was hidden in that space?

"Yo—Landa!" Tony brayed, from down at the desk. "Where're you hiding Book Baby? I know you're in here. You never buy lunch or leave to hit the ladies room. So, what I want to know is...what do you do with your poo?"

"Some of us aren't as full of it as you are," Yolanda answered, from the balcony where she had apparently been released from her spell by Tony's crass levity. "We might have a climber up here. I'm trying to flush him out. Guard the stairways down there to grab him if he makes a run for it."

"Sweet! Finally some excitement in this morgue!"

Of course, Yolanda did no such thing. She went back to the section with the haunted book. The whole bookcase held multiple editions of the works of Lewis Carroll. *Alice's Adventures, Through the Looking Glass, Hunting the Snark,* and *Sylvie and Bruno* were all there in more than enough editions and languages to choke a *Jabberwocky.* She found them easy to remove from the shelves, but hiding nothing except the metal backing of the bookcase. However, at the back of the bottom shelf, where the cumulative weight of all those books had stressed the seams in the metal, a small sliver of dim light shone through.

On hands and knees, pressing her face into the space reserved for books, she could feel cold air and detect a rank odor issuing from the small opening. With her eye pressed to the metal, she thought she could make out a chair leg and nothing more. She resolved to return tomorrow with a plan to enter that hidden space.

o——o

The next day became the longest Yolanda had ever experienced. She discovered the new sensation of "killing time" in the Collections, and time stubbornly refused to die. This offered her a mercifully brief glimpse into Tony's mindset with his jokes and daydreams as well as Dr. Gray's compulsive management and promotion activities—mostly carried on outside the Collections' confines. Yolanda's thwarted desires had never been to escape the Collections and embrace outside connections. They focused on tunneling deeper into the Collections, discarding the outside world with all its disappointing complications.

Aside from a group of geriatric females, who sought "authentic" information on covens, patron traffic remained nonexistent. Dr. Gray and her lap dog Tony, scurried around rearranging things for the coming exhibit. Yolanda found it virtually impossible to stay at her desk and excruciating to resist the gravitational pull of the mezzanine's tantalizing mysteries.

She got permission from Dr. Gray to mop the dust off the mezzanine floors, even though this was clearly housekeeping's job. Doing so had the double benefit of soothing Yolanda's overwhelming need to study the suspect area and to remove the telltale possibilities of past and future footprints.

The rest of the day, she found herself drawn time and again to the large portrait of John Griswold White, which hung at the west end of the room. It presented a strange, indistinct depiction. An extremely elderly gentleman seated at a document-strewn writing desk, responding to some intruder (arguably the artist, Sandor Vago), with a troubled expression.

"Are you all right?" inquired Dr. Gray, after noticing her fixation with the picture. "You seem edgy today. You're normally more...well, sedentary."

"I'm fine. Ol' Gris visited me yesterday when you and Tony went out."

"Please stop talking like that," Dr. Gray begged. "Don't we have enough of those horridly-dressed Goth types coming in here researching ghosts and witches? God knows how long it's been since anyone actually inquired about chess."

"Sorry, Shelly. Do you know what happened to this old guy?"

"Died, I presume," Dr. Gray replied. "I mean everyone must—eventually. His family crypt is located in Lakeview Cemetery. You should visit him out there and stop arranging your meetings in the Collections. You know how it creeps me out!"

o——o

That evening as the announcement of closing time sounded in the

Main Library, Tony and Dr. Gray hit the elevator running. Yolanda expected to lock up the Special Collections areas as she did every evening, since she liked being the last to leave. Lock up she did, but in reverse, launching her clandestine plan. Carrying her especially loaded bag of tools to the first set of gates, she closed them, stuck her arm through the ornate bars and turned the lock from outside. Then she switched off the lights in the exhibit corridor, walked back inside the second gates, and repeated this reverse ritual.

With the lights off in the Collections room, she made her way carefully under the stairwell chain and up to the mezzanine aisle. As long as she remained relatively quiet and kept the beam from her newly purchased work light from spilling into the main Collections room— she could remain undiscovered by the night guard walking his rounds down the main corridors.

Excited in a way she had never experienced before, she began her careful assault on the mysterious bookshelf and what it concealed.

"All right Ol' Gris, show me your door," she whispered to herself, as she carefully removed the books from the vicinity of the open seam. The bookcases were all metal, six shelves high with upright walls roughly three feet apart. Each bookcase section bolted to the next with its metal back screwed into the wall. However, in the suspect area, two sections had been welded together and showed no sign how their backing plates were secured.

On close inspection, the far upright of one section hid a concealed piano hinge running from floor to ceiling. On the opposite side of the next section the books smack up against the upright proved to be false volumes that could not be removed, cunningly disguised as obscure works in unlikely languages.

"What is this?" she silently asked her unseen companion.

"Think about it," he replied in her mind. "Only an exceptional girl like you would have come even this far."

If the welded double sections comprised the entrance and the hinges worked, she reasoned, *then the door must open out. That meant the opposite edge must be beveled backward to allow the deep shelves to swing open. The false books hide this otherwise obvious bevel.* She felt close now, but no amount of quiet force applied to the empty sections caused the slightest movement.

"Where's the lock?" she asked in hushed tones.

"Where should it be?" he taunted gently.

Standing directly in front of the hypothetical door, Yolanda let her hand touch the volumes in the next bookcase. At precisely the location where one might expect a knob or latch, she found a thick edition of Scheherazade's *A Thousand and One Arabian Nights.*

"Open sesame," she whispered, as she attempted to draw the book out. She heard a muffled *click* and saw a small puff of long settled dust, as the double section moved slightly.

Pulling the section open with some difficulty, Yolanda faced the momentary specter of the old gentleman turning to confront her from his littered desk, just as in his portrait. This quickly proved to be purely a figment of Yolanda's inflamed imagination. The dim moonlight creeping into the cluttered oblong room through a pair of small south-facing windows fell instead on the remains of the legendary benefactor himself. His withered corpse sat forever enthralled by a thick portfolio, spread across his moldering desk. Without invitation, Yolanda carefully slipped inside to join him.

Ol' Gris' desk, chair, and desiccated corpse dominated the interior of the room. The surrounding walls were lined with shelves full of books, manuscripts, and maps; the floor littered with even more.

31

Everything lay coated with thick dust and flakes of peeled paint. The room felt like a refrigerator even though the rest of the library maintained a comfortable temperature. In one corner, water dripped from a cracked window. Yolanda located numerous burnt-out candles and an empty kerosene lamp, but could find no indication the room ever had electricity.

With the batteries in her work light dying, she completed her first cursory examination of the room. She had failed to bring more and lost track of the time already spent in this mesmerizing time capsule of knowledge and death.

"What a shame," his voice whispered. "I have so much more to show you."

"I'll come back," she said.

"Will they let you," he questioned, planting seeds of infectious doubt in her mind.

Yolanda had not actually thought about that. She had pondered what she would find and how to find it, but success beyond her wildest fantasies proved another matter. The difficulties of sharing her discovery or hiding it now flooded her faculties. Her self-doubts floated to the top with the probable answer. She wouldn't be able do either. Shelly and Tony would steal everything away from her. They would make the room a centerpiece of their damned exhibit. Dr. Gray would get a promotion, and Tony would use the spotlight of notoriety to do nothing more worthy than chase tail. Yolanda would never have a moment's peace in the Collections again...never get to absorb all the mysteries that she, and she alone, had discovered.

"Or," he purred. "You could stay here. I want to show you the book."

"In this room?" she shuddered. "With you?"

"Why not? They never have to know. All this is ours now."

With less than two hours before the library opened, Yolanda worked feverishly. She replaced all the books on the camouflaged door in perfect order. She cleaned the floor of the aisle and removed hand and fingerprints. As the first slivers of dawn started to streak the sky outside, she stepped back into their secret room and drew the door closed behind her. With a soft *click* of the hidden lock, she vanished safely inside.

"Let's listen to the fools looking for you," he snickered, as she crouched in silence with her ear to the door.

o——o

After the initial shock of not finding Yolanda at her habitual post, Dr. Gray and Tony recovered reasonably well. Shelly dug up her own set of keys and Tony had to ride the desk. They expected Yolanda to show up late or at least call. When she did neither, Dr. Gray got her number from Human Resources. She was prepared to offer sympathy, assistance, or even a loan if necessary...anything to get Yolanda back to work ASAP.

o——o

Daylight flooding into the sealed room revealed the multitude of wonders Yolanda had found. Volumes and manuscripts that disappeared from the Collections generations ago materialized on these shelves. Even the legendary work on witchcraft purporting to include the Devil's actual handwriting lay open for her perusal.

"Obvious fakery," Ol' Gris huffed. "But the penalties for counterfeiting the Dark One's hand proved appallingly real indeed."

The most enticing of all the room's displays was a huge world map attached to the back of the bookcase door. Thousands of cryptically annotated dots of increasingly sinister colors were laced together with an intricate net of traced converging lines.

"My web of connotation," he whispered.

"What does it mean?"

"Each dot is a procured source. Each line is where its content led me."

"Ending in these black dots," she concluded.

"Yes," he hissed. "The source of all, compiled from all the ages and cultures of the world into this." His voice led her to the open portfolio gathering dust on the desk in the grip of his rotted skeletal fingers.

"All about the game of chess?" she guessed.

"Hah," his laugh echoed in the room as if coming from the crumbling teeth and jaws of his corpse. "Don't be the fool I was! I wasted decades looking the wrong way, from chess forward in time to all its meanings and metaphors."

"Instead of...?"

"Seeing the game itself represented a metaphor...a visualization of the primal struggle of light and darkness. For the origins of that struggle you must search backward in time, past the crusades, the Persians, the Israelites to the absolute beginnings of men and beyond."

o——o

After the failure to contact Yolanda, the difficulties of mounting the new exhibit shorthanded drew all focus. The primary concern became that she had gone missing with a set of keys to the Collections. Compensating padlocks appeared on the gates and chains until time and money could be found to rekey the antique brass locks, which themselves constituted a part of the John Griswold White legacy.

Sometime during this confusion of priorities, old George the security guard took responsibility himself to search Yolanda's apartment. He considered her a friend, a daughter almost, and felt he had failed in his duty to protect her. The condition of her apartment, with no sign of travel preparations, and cluttered with piles of unfinished abandoned manuscripts, confirmed the suspicious nature of her unexplained absence. George filed a missing persons report with the Cleveland Police. At the time, women disappeared in Cleveland at an alarming rate. Many were discovered murdered in abandoned houses, but some simply ceased to exist. George was determined that Yolanda would not be one of them.

o——o

"The book is called *The History of the Elder Gods,*" Ol' Gris explained. "Precious few copies exist. They're incredibly rare and carefully guarded. But, remnants and translations of random pages were available. I searched the globe for them, paid enormous sums, and ordered unspeakable deeds to obtain them. Now I have them all collected here, the complete text, of enormous portent and infinite value, but useless to me now."

"Why useless?" Yolanda hungered to know.

"Because I couldn't live long enough to understand it, and neither shall you."

Yolanda pried the open portfolio of loose pages from the corpse's grasp. The illustrations were disturbing and repulsive. Images of horror deified and triumphant played across the moldy pages. Surely the text would explain all this madness, but that was the primary source of his lamentation. The pages existed in hundreds of languages, most long dead and many nameless and unknown. They would take lifetimes to decipher. Universities of scholars could make careers of trying to comprehend this unholy diabolical work.

The task was hopeless. Yolanda laid her head down on the undecipherable pages in defeat. She thought of her thwarted obsession to author a great work of her own. Here in her grasp was the greatest story never told, a saga so deep and inexpressible only the Gods themselves dare read it. From her despair, born in the dark unknowable boundaries between desire and fulfillment, the meanings began to come to her, to seep up from the pages moistened with her tears, through her skin, via her surging bloodstream, and into her fevered mind.

Possibly she *could* understand this forbidden text. Not with her eyes, but through her touch. Absorb it. Let it flood her inner being and drown her puny humanity in its dark foreboding monstrosity. She must become one with this eldritch lore by the most intimate of contact. She placed her mouth on the swirling undecipherable script and extended her tongue.

"Clever girl," Ol' Gris chuckled. "I'd never thought of that."

o——o

Security cameras showed no record of Yolanda leaving the library on the night she disappeared. The police organized a massive after-hours search of the entire complex. They concentrated on all the hidden out-of-the-way places just big enough to hide a body. After several long nights of failure they called the search off. The over-extended municipal force could only expend so much time and manpower on any one disappearance, before being forced to move on to the next and the next. Appallingly, that pipeline never ran dry.

Still George refused to give up. If she wasn't in the Main Library, then she must still be in the Collections itself. He haunted this section for days whenever his duties allowed. Dr. Gray and Tony came to resent his relentless questioning, exposing as it did their casual disinterest in Yolanda's life and fate.

Finally George discovered some faint inexplicable trace on the floor of a mezzanine aisle. It appeared some heavy object had dragged or rolled in an arc across the wooden floor. After gaining permission from management to stay in the Collections overnight, George discovered the hidden room by following an almost imperceptible mewing and mumbling which seemed to issue from the solid walls. The night maintenance crew helped him find and dismantle the hidden door.

They found Yolanda filthy, emaciated, and feral—curled up in the boney lap of John Griswold White's rotted corpse; her mind incurably destroyed by the toxic pigments, inks, and mold from an unidentifiable portfolio—which she devoured completely.

HUNT & GATHER

(The Flats—Cuyahoga Valley National Park)

Some people have all the luck. If that includes "bad luck"—the type contorting an otherwise perfectly normal existence and bending its trajectory ever downward—then Dave was such a person.

An indifferent childhood, iffy education, and unfortunate choices were all part of his problem. But actually it was something else, something inevitable. The fault, as they say, "was in his stars."

He'd done a creditable job of avoiding disaster. You couldn't say he succumbed without a fight. After all, he was married, gainfully employed, and marginally content before events defeated him. That dark night something broke inside him—something vital, irreplaceable, and apparently dangerous.

We won't go into how his marriage ended, his job evaporated, and his finances drained. There was plenty of that going around. The "Great Recession," banking malfeasance, and "War on Terror" pretty much squeezed the juices out of his entire generation, especially here in Cleveland. Most others found a way to bounce back or at least soldier on—but not Dave.

You could invoke the possibility of substance abuse and mental aberration, but even if these were present, they still couldn't explain his downfall entirely. Let's just say he "crossed over," and here's how it all went down.

Dave was drinking at Hoopple's bar on the West Bank of the Flats. The Cleveland Indians lost again and were in the process of setting up permanent housekeeping in the cellar of their division. The Tea Party, concealed-carry, and right-to-work fanatics also drinking there tore the conversational guts out of every liberal delusion Dave still cherished. Closing time caught him drunk and nodding off at the bar.

Outside in the deserted parking lot, his car had been vandalized into immobile junk and he dropped and stepped on his cell phone trying to call a cab.

As he staggered northward along the abandoned section of Riverbed Street, a neighborhood chapter of the "Heartless Felons" gang chanced upon him. After beating the piss out of him just for laughs, they stole his wallet, keys, everything else in his pockets, and smashed his glasses. Then it started to pour down rain.

Somewhat later, Dave wandered up under the east end of the Veterans Memorial Bridge for shelter. He found a trash barrel ablaze and the vague promise of warmth drew him in. Three resident home-less squatters barred his access to their cozy circle and demanded cigarettes as admission. Of course, Dave had none. That's when one of them grabbed his jacket instead.

What happened next was never clear to Dave. There was a great deal of profanity, loud screaming, and a prolonged fit of vigorous ac-tivity involving a jagged chunk of concrete. Afterward, Dave crawled up close to the warmth of the stinking trash fire and passed out.

The next morning a vicious hangover could not blunt the horrible discovery of congealed slaughter surrounding him. Dave's torn and gory jacket told him more about the night's proceedings than he cared to remember. This was the end. He had finally bottomed out and sat placidly among his pulverized victims awaiting discovery and incar-ceration.

By noon it became apparent the universe remained so indifferent to his fate, he must obtain even his own apprehension and punish-ment. That made him laugh. Dave laughed and laughed, and sometime during this spasm of cathartic hilarity his victims' shattered jaws and mangled tongues joined in the frivolity.

At that moment, Dave stepped out of himself and into a new domain; a world with no rules or morals, a life without constraints on impulse or desire. Dave existed free in that world now, eternally exonerated from all reason or consequence. He stood, dusted himself off, removed his brain-splattered jacket, and tossed it to the three silent witnesses to his resurrection. "Here boys," he said. "You can keep it. I've got things to do."

o———o

"Oh, God," moaned veteran detective MacDonald, as he shielded his nose from the pervasive stench. "Sometimes I feel like such a dinosaur."

"What you moanin' about?" asked his young partner, Jamal, as he poked delicately through the carnage with a long stick. "I'm down here workin' the yucky stuff."

MacDonald gazed around wistfully at the handful of gawkers gathering on the far side of the crime tape. The evidence team photographed shot after shot of the confusion of muddy shoeprints radiating from the splatter zone. The situation made MacDonald want to vomit, but he kept it down out of long practice.

"This murder business used to be logical," MacDonald said. "With clues and suspects and...motives. Remember comprehensible motives, Jamal? Now everything's senseless and random."

Jamal stepped gingerly around the jumble of bloody clothing and entangled corpses looking for anything that didn't quite fit—like searching for a corner piece in a jigsaw puzzle from which he could begin to reconstruct the whole picture.

"Uh huh, I recall that," Jamal answered. "Sometime things still go like that in the burbs. But down here—with these street folks—things be different. You still got perps and breadcrumbs leadin' off to reasons why. It's just hard 'cause you can't think like them. 'Cause you and me don't live like them. But the shit's all here somewhere...like lookie, lookie what I found!"

Jamal's stick fished out a torn jacket splattered with dried blood and tissue fragments. Each stinking fragment attracted a small galaxy of swarming maggots and green bottle flies.

"What've we got?" MacDonald sighed.

"This here jacket don't seem to belong on any of these dead folk, but these flies show it was here for the party."

"So the owner of this jacket is probably our guy," mused MacDonald. "Seems possible, but still doesn't give us why."

"Why is tough," Jamal said, shrugging his shoulders with indifference. "Could be somebody panhandled on somebody else's turf. Could be these guys disrespected the wrong crack head up the hill at St. Malachi's soup kitchen. Or could be—"

"It could be they just tore his damned jacket," groaned MacDonald. "Why Jamal? Why would anybody smash a guy's skull...no, three guys' skulls over a torn jacket? And why in God's name, would he keep doing that over and over again until he turned them all into *Jello*?"

"Why? That part be easy, Mack," Jamal joked, going into his best Bill Cosby impersonation. "Cause nobody don't love *JELL-O*!"

○——○

In Dave's new world planning ahead proved difficult. After all, anything was possible, and nothing was forbidden. This provided infinite choices, but no criteria by which to choose. Eventually the base necessities dictated events: Dave got hungry.

He walked up to a random door on Clinton Avenue and knocked. An older woman came to the door. She reminded Dave of somebody's grandmother.

"Could you help me?" he said. "I've had nothing to eat today." She opened the door partially, but when she saw the mud caked on his shoes and pants she hesitated. Dave grabbed her by the throat and dragged her back inside.

After the killing, which proved easier than he could ever have imagined, Dave positioned her gently on the sofa in the living room and covered her up to the chin with a comforter from the hall closet. She appeared peaceful, which pleased Dave in some way. Then he went into her kitchen and made some bacon, eggs-over-easy, and toast. Coffee sat already brewing, for which Dave felt vaguely grateful.

After eating, Dave wandered about the house taking mental inventory of all it contained. This was all his now—if he wanted. It amused him to imagine all the decades of hard work, thrift, and sacrifice the house represented. All free now. It was a joke really. The pursuits and priorities of his former life and hers and everyone else's became just one huge waste of time.

A car pulled up to the curb in front of the house. Through a window, Dave saw a middle-aged man get out and walk up to the front door. Dave made some quick adjustments in the living room, then went to answer the knocking.

"Who are you?" asked the man.

"A friend from the neighborhood," Dave lied.

"I've never met you before."

"That makes two of us."

"Where's my mother?"

"She's laying down on the sofa. I don't think she's feeling well." This seemed to alarm her son. Dave opened the door and allowed him to pass on toward the living room. Dave followed, and when the son bent down to check on his mother's condition, Dave crushed his skull with the base of a heavy table lamp he unplugged moments earlier for just such a purpose.

Now there were two bodies on the sofa and Dave had a change of clothes and a car as his reward. *Great,* Dave thought. *That was easy.*

o———o

Three days after the homeless massacre, MacDonald had a set of probable fingerprints, possible DNA, and a tentative set of shoeprints leading in and out of the crime scene. The jacket was standard off-the-rack sportswear and therefore untraceable. His investigation remained active but going nowhere when Jamal called in, claiming the uniformed boys had found his guy a dozen blocks from the bridge. The jaded veteran doubted it could be that easy, but sometimes they lucked out and caught a break. He prayed silently during the drive over this was one of those times.

"Why do you think it's him?" MacDonald asked, standing beside Jamal in the victim's living room.

"'Cause the mud, the shoes, and them pants match our jacket...minus the flies and such," answered Jamal, as the evidence team sniffed out the rest of the house around them.

"But he's dead, Jamal, seated nice-as-you-please on a couch holding hands with some other old stiff," MacDonald pointed out. "How'd that happen?"

"Neighbors say she's his mother. He's devoted to her. Visited twice a week at least."

"Very thoughtful. How'd he buy it?"

"Crushed skull, used this lamp to brain himself. It's got yuck all over the bottom.

"Well, that fits the MO. Her too?"

"Nope," Jamal said. "Strangled her. Check out them bruises on her neck. I'm guessin' some sorta weird murder/suicide thing with a side order of *Psycho* thrown in. What you think, Mack?"

"Well, we can check out the shoes, the mud, his DNA, and the fingerprints on her neck, but I'm betting our guy walked away."

"How so?"

"Because the clothes don't really fit this guy, do they Jamal? They're a bit too small. Nothing is buttoned up all the way. Our guy staged all this—the sick bastard."

"Why'd he do that?"

"I don't know! Maybe he thinks it's funny. Maybe he's taunting us, showing off how frigging clueless we are about his next move," MacDonald fumed.

"What're we gonna do?"

"Investigate, damn it! He's wearing different clothes that are hanging a little loose. He's probably driving this poor bastard's car and… and…what else did he take?"

"Not much, a free breakfast, a shower, and a big shit in the upstairs bathroom," answered Jamal. "He forgot to flush."

o——o

By that time, Dave moved to the country in search of serenity to contemplate his new condition. He'd chosen a semi-secluded farmstead in the Cuyahoga Valley National Park that runs south of the city along the river. He found the location by stopping for peaches at a little roadside produce stand run by the farmer's wife.

After strangling her, Dave killed her two children when they were delivered up to him by their yellow school bus, and finally the farmer himself back from a hard day of work in his pickup truck. They all sat now in the car stolen on Clinton Avenue, arranged like a happily deceased family off to a summer outing, but parked out of sight in the barn going nowhere ever again.

Dave experienced a long dormant need while wrestling the last breath out of the wife. While not an attractive woman, he used her body anyway and achieved relief without any hint of pleasure. The children proved more difficult as he had some moments to ponder their playful antics before deciding how to kill them. He chose drowning in a duck pond behind the house, as this left no ugly marks on their precious faces. By the time the farmer arrived home, Dave discovered the house held hunting rifles, knives, and a double-bladed axe—so he had more options.

Dave now slept in the couple's bed, fed their pets, and contemplated the empty stillness of their comfy home. The pointlessness of home and family haunted him along with the useless nature of ideas such as happiness, love, and even human reproduction itself. These things meant nothing to him now. Books and television proved incomprehensible. Without empathy or even mere curiosity, everything became meaningless patterns of light and shadow. He found himself drawn instead to the tangled woods of the parkland, precisely because they existed free of ill-conceived human notions of purpose or order.

Stalking the woods devolved him. He entered the animal realm and kept off the park trails entirely. He even tried removing his shoes and socks to better ground himself in primeval sensibility, but his lack of calluses failed him. From the depths of leafy seclusion, he watched unwary humanity cavort or idle along without the slightest notion of what lurked only yards away. Seeing them as prey or even less, Dave still refrained from action because they offered nothing to him now. Even the bouncing cleavage of the young joggers no longer caused sensation.

Then he came upon a lone fly fisherman in hip boots wading in the shallows of the river. Dave thought to himself, *I liked to fish.*

o———o

Technically, the National Park fell under the jurisdiction of the Rangers who policed with the help of the Ohio State Highway Patrol. But since the victims were found in a car Cleveland police were searching for in connection with multiple homicides, Jamal and Mack found themselves in the barn confronting their latest known failure to "protect and serve."

"It's always hard when they do the kids," Jamal lamented, nose pressed against the car window for closer inspection.

"And rape their mothers," MacDonald added.

"How you know that?"

"Very few women dress for a family outing wearing nothing below the waist."

Macdonald wandered out of the barn where the evidence frenzy was about to begin and stood in the fading light of dusk. Jamal came up behind him reading his probable mood by the defeated slump of his shoulders.

"We ain't ever catchin' up, are we?"

"Not if he keeps moving. He's like a shark swimming through a school of herring. He just chomps and swims, and chomps and swims, and so on...until he decides to stop, runs out of herring, or somebody manages to chomp back. Any way it goes, you and I will always show up just in time to tidy up the mess. We might as well be janitors."

"Don't be down like that, Mack. You'll think of somethin'."

"Right now, I'm thinking about getting something to eat," MacDonald said. "The state boys are in charge of checking the site. They'll tell us what they find. The family pickup is still here so there's a chance he's in the area. The Rangers will stake the place out in case he returns. Who knows, our problem could be all over tonight, and you and I can sleep like babies."

o——o

Dave's fishing yielded him nothing but proof even habitual activity provided no satisfaction. Returning the rod and reel to its submerged owner pinned to the bottom under large rocks, Dave slunk away once again into the forest and prowled back toward the farm.

He sat concealed in the undergrowth, watching the bustle of authorities swarming the property with bemused interest. For the first time since his transformation, Dave imagined others might be following his progress. *Why do they bother?* he thought. For the slightest moment he considered surrender. He experienced no enjoyment in what transpired inside him or its grisly consequences—so why not end it? Then Dave realized the police offered no end to his ordeal, only a long ritual search for explanations. He had none...so he moved on.

A new dynamic now animated him, the thrill of the chased. A half-mile north of the farmhouse he came upon a sheltered area of the towpath trail. Lunging from ambush upon a lone cyclist, Dave slit the rider's throat with a single fluid motion of the farmer's borrowed hunting knife and rolled the spandex-wrapped body down into a thicket of vines and poison ivy. Mounting the bike, Dave peddled furiously northward on the pathway toward increased anonymity in the glowing neon anthill of downtown Cleveland.

o——o

"I'm thinking about our guy," MacDonald said, as he nursed his whiskey and waited for their dinner to arrive at the new flats eatery owned by the Metroparks.

"Oh, yeah," said Jamal, surfing the Internet on his smart phone. "You and everyone else in town. Lookie here, the *Plain Dealer* says,

'*Madman Terrorizes Cleveland—Police Baffled by Murder Spree.*' You think that's true, Mack? You think we're baffled by this guy?"

MacDonald let out a long painful sigh and took a thoughtful sip on his whiskey. "No, I think this guy is baffled. We can't figure out what he's doing because he doesn't know himself. We can't know why or who or where because he doesn't know either."

"Is that why he's mad—'cause he don't know? The news is full of killin' and rapin' every day," Jamal reasoned, showing Mack his phone screen as he scrolled through a list of local atrocities. "We don't call that madness. We call that criminal."

"I don't know what madness is," Mack said. "Could be you have to go mad to know mad, and I'm not quite there yet. Let's just try to have a decent meal and a few drinks like normal people and talk about something else."

"Like sports? Whatta you think about them Cleveland Brownies, Mack?"

"Oh, Hell no! That would drive me crazy!"

o——o

The towpath trail dead-ended at Merwin's Wharf, a semi-plush new eatery constructed by the Park Department to cash in on the re-birth of the East bank of the Flats. Dave arrived after dark, worn out and hungry from his long ride. Leaving the bike in a rack with others, he walked in. Money taken from the old woman, her son, the farmer, and the produce stand stuffed his pockets. So he shook off his feral ways, sat down, and ordered by nods and pointing, creeping out the restaurant staff with his silent expressionless demeanor and ragged appearance.

His lack of interaction was symptomatic of mounting detachment from the world around him. But it wasn't complete. His almost catatonic state of mental vacuity had a flaw. He could not stop hearing. The confused chatter of the other diners leaked into his consciousness and filled his mind to overflowing. Each conversation reverberated in acute clarity, but near total incomprehension, as all mixed together into babble.

As he had no thoughts of his own, the thoughts of others floated in and out of focus. His food came and he ate. Somewhere between the meat and potatoes he recognized a thread of conversation. An older white man seated with a younger black man at a distant table seemed to be talking about him, or more precisely about someone doing grotesque things he vaguely remembered experiencing.

This troubling self-recognition expanded exponentially until every voice seemed to refer to his activity. The pressure of sorting through so many imagined memories overcame him. He stopped eating, placed all his money on the half-emptied plate, got up, and walked into the restroom.

In the empty restroom the voices subsided and Dave could relieve himself without further disorientation. However, when he stepped up to the sink the mirror image staring back at him was unrecognizable. Either Dave forgot how he looked, changed appearance during his ordeal, or only now experienced a lack of vision traceable to the loss of his long-forgotten glasses. His identity crisis deepened as he began to see multiple images. First the mangled homeless appeared, then the old woman, her son, and eventually all the rest. The mirror filled with faces reflecting a restroom crammed with dead humanity, all indistinguishable from Dave himself.

Fleeing the empty restroom, Dave hurried out onto the patio running along the riverbank. Pleasure boats of all sizes were moored there as their owners dined. Dave imagined himself in those boats, floating down the river and out into the vast dark lake beyond. This calming fantasy of seclusion became a need. He would continue across the lake and on into Canada. The sheltering pines would embrace him, absorbing him in their snowy evergreen silence. Last would come the icy emptiness of the arctic. Dave would disappear forever into frozen crystalline solitude.

Dave boarded an empty cabin cruiser and wandered about the deck attempting to imagine how he could release and control it, as he had no nautical experience whatsoever. An inebriated shirtless man came out of the cabin holding a beer can. He confronted Dave against the boat's railing, facing out onto the dark brown water flowing slowly downriver.

"Hey buddy," he said. "What do you think...?" But stopped mid-sentence while experiencing (however briefly) the once-in-a-lifetime sensation of a large hunting knife plunging into his chest. Dave supported the man's weight, removed the beer can from his dead grasp, and gracefully allowed the body to slip over the rail and slide head first into the murky water with a nearly inaudible "slosh." Not having tasted alcohol since drinking at Hoopples, Dave sat on a deck chair and finished the man's beverage.

While Dave sat contemplating how to operate his new craft, a commotion arose farther down the waterfront. The shirtless man's body became entangled in a departing boat's propeller. This discovery elicited a loud reaction, drawing a crowd from the restaurant, including the two men Dave had initially found troubling.

Dave abandoned his improbable voyage, got off the boat, and made toward the bike racks. A pair of Park Department vehicles blocked the racks with multiple rangers examining the bike he so recently borrowed. The situation seemed inescapable, but Dave simply re-boarded the cabin cruiser, lowered himself over the far side of the boat, and slid silently into the dark cool water.

Floating across the river like a nearly submerged crocodile, Dave felt his way along the overgrown West Bank of the river until he passed unseen in the night past the grisly situation of the propeller, around the bend, and out of sight. Across from the old grain elevators Dave dragged himself out of the Cuyahoga River using low hanging branches and vines. He struggled up the steep wooded bank until finding himself once again soaked to the skin on Riverbed Street.

Whether Dave realized he had come full circle is unimportant. Perhaps it felt familiar or inevitable. Whatever his perception he found his way to the trash barrel under the bridge, which again burned savagely in the night.

Being alone this time, Dave removed his shoes and soaked clothing. He arranged them neatly around the fire to dry. Thus naked and unarmed, he encountered the Heartless Felons for the second time. Of course, even trapped in this vulnerable condition, Dave was not now the docile drunken stooge he had been before, and the Felons sensed this.

But tonight, the Felons were not looking to beat and rob. Tonight they planed to stage an initiation. Prospective gang wanabees had to prove their heartless status before joining. The trash barrel was lit off to attract suitable victims for this ritual, like attracting moths to a flame. Three young boys stepped out of the gang and confronted Dave. Two held what seemed to be water balloons and the third carried a familiar long stick tipped with a knotted oily rag.

Dave made a desperate feint to one side seeking escape, but was pelted by bursting balloons which soaked his hair, face, and body. The liquid burned his eyes and mouth. His nostrils were assaulted by the sharp odor of gasoline. The third boy lit his torch in the trash fire, threw it, and Dave became illuminated.

The initial effect on Dave is difficult to describe. Certainly the pain was not instantaneous. The long seconds between ignition and incineration were more about shock, strange exhilaration, and even revelations of a dire sort. In any case, Dave did not react as any previous Felon sacrifice had. There was no screaming, running around, or frantic attempts to smother the flames.

Instead, Dave stood transfixed with his gaze and arms stretched hopelessly skyward. As the hair and flesh began to burn away and blacken, he let out one impossibly long soulful bellow of despair. This spooked the heart out of even the Felons, who fled the spectacle into the far corners of the night. Then, in the excruciating void between life and death, Dave achieved the absolute polar opposite of enlightenment. He became not one with everything, but melted down into not much at all.

"Oh, God please," moaned MacDonald, shielding his nose from the lingering stench of burnt flesh, as Jamal poked at the charred remains with that same damned stick. "Please, not this again."

OFF RAMP

(The Shoreway—Dead Man's Curve)

After college and some lean years failing to make a living in the arts, I took work pushing orange plastic barrels. They called it *traffic control*. Road repair, which required only a few painted metal drums and kerosene lanterns for protection before 1950, exploded with the construction of the high-speed interstates. Building new superhighways seemed easy. But to maintain them decades on—as concrete cracked, asphalt buckled, and I-beams rusted under the onslaught of ballooning traffic—took a whole new industrial art form.

It was all about maintaining "the flow." Suburbanites had to come and go daily like the tides. Rush hours, traffic lanes, and high speeds were the new imperatives. Body count was peripheral. Roadwork became more dangerous than coal mining.

We were out on the east shoreway, running a three-mile zone westbound for a night asphalt-resurfacing job. Four lanes squeezed left into one, with a movable off ramp to downtown located right at Dead Man's Curve. Old Joe, "the Bermwalker," ran the show with "Whitey" Wilkes, Sam "the Hammer" Green, and me providing the manual labor.

Our work had been living hell earlier with traffic sandwiched between the center barrier wall and our barrel line. Only two measly feet of shoulder existed on the left against the wall, and we were stealing two-and-a-half back with our barrels on the right to allow the paving machines to reach the lane lines. The fine motorists of Cleveland did not take kindly to this vehicular claustrophobia.

Now at nearly 3 a.m., Cleveland was a ghost city. The remaining hard-core drunks closing down the bars mostly headed east out of town. We road workers were down at the notorious curve, moving the off-ramp back and forth by shifting signs and barrels as the paving machines and rollers worked their way up and down each lane. The stench of dead lake fish and hot asphalt turned the humid summer air into a pungent stew.

So many overhead highway lights were broken or shot out, we worked by moonlight and the occasional passing headlights. The darkness and desolation of that manmade wasteland was oppressive. Ten hours into a sixteen-hour shift, the asphalt trucks tended to run late. We had time to kill, but little energy left to use it.

I stared up at the smoke stacks of the electrical power plant as gray billows of steam and ash poured out and blew overhead. The pollution watchdogs were in bed because the Feds don't do overtime, and every industry knew it. This fine rain of filth left a crusty residue at the edges of our eyes, mouths, and nostrils.

"Where the hell is everybody?" I asked.

"What you mean?" asked the Hammer. "We's all here 'ceptin' the Bermwalker. He's sleepin' in his truck, like always."

"I mean where are all the damn people, the motorists who pay for this road? It's like they all died off and we're stuck out here doing this for nothing."

"You're gettin' paid, ain't you?" sneered Whitey, our resident, ill-tempered, hill-jack scarecrow.

"I hope so," I said. "I'd hate to think we're the last living souls on duty while everyone else has left the planet. Maybe we missed *the rapture.*"

"What's this rapture talk?" the Hammer asked. "What's that mean?"

"Well…" I started, before Whitey cut me off.

"Spiderman don't know shit 'bout that. Just cause he went to college, he thinks he can hold forth on any damn thing!"

"Then you explain it," I said.

"I don't need to," claimed Whitey. "I'm born-again Baptist. If 'in there was a rapture I'd know it—'cause I wouldn't be standin' here jabberin' with you fools!" Whitey's assumptions were legion. Possibly he had a valid point, if he wasn't overestimating his own piety or discounting ours. We spent several long moments standing silently in the dark while all around us the vacancy of all other living things seemed to expand out into the suffocating night.

"Still," I said, after a sufficiently respectful interlude. "We do seem to be all alone. I bet I could walk out into the open lane and just stand there for ten or fifteen minutes without a single car running me over."

"Go ahead," Whitey huffed. "Only a damn fool like you would try it."

"I'll do it with you, Spiderman," said the Hammer, smiling a toothy grin. "Let's put money on it. Ten bucks says I stays out longer than you."

The Hammer was a betting man. He played the lotto religiously and spent weekends at the track, much to the detriment of his ever increasing and loosely related offspring. But I had ten bucks and losing it wouldn't kill me. So we shook on it and both stepped out into the open lane facing east toward approaching destiny.

"You two are nuts!" yelled Whitey, with a nasty trail of chewing tobacco dribbling down his chin. "Whattabout them asphalt trucks? How'd you feel with eighteen wheels an shit-loads of asphalt rollin' over your smart asses?"

"They're running inside the zone," I said. "More likely to kill you than us." The Hammer laughed and we returned to our suicide stance. Standing side by side, his ebony shoulders came up even with my head. Our bet wasn't about dominance, this genial giant could crush me like a bug and the money was only an excuse. It was a test of...

something else. Something serious men seek and lesser souls avoid.

It wasn't long in starting. Somewhere out near MLK Boulevard, we caught the sweep of lights coming around the curves. Whitey started to laugh.

"Ain't been five minutes," he taunted. The Hammer's eyes went wide. Now we would see. But onrushing death was still miles away— plenty of time to get religion and chicken out. When the lights came even with the power plant by East 55th street we could tell it was no car. The headlights set too high, and the engine growl belonged to a powerful diesel. The Hammer faked a lunge toward the barrel line, but I did not bite. I would not make this easy for either of us. At one hundred yards away the driver must have seen the reflection from our safety vests. His brakes squealed as he scrubbed off speed and dipped behind the barrel line, redeeming us both.

"Asphalt truck," I said, as Whitey watched it pass behind him, "in the zone as expected."

"That was fun!" said the Hammer. "Let's double down Spiderman."

"I don't have the money," I confessed.

"Don't need none," he said with a sly grin, while turning around to face west. Thus blind to danger's approach, the stakes grew higher.

"Is that all you got?" I asked, turning to match his daring. Now the Hammer dropped his grin. He did not like to lose, especially to some punk like me. I could see him weighing the odds—his boldness against my crazy. But nobody, including me, knew the full extent of that.

"You think you're bad?" he asked. "I'll show you bad, college boy." Then he lay down on the highway, stretching out to his full length, flat on his back, with his arms folded casually under his head as if sun bathing by starlight.

This was a very, very bad idea—stupid, absurdly dangerous, and daring the Devil himself to intervene. That's why I admired it. I felt as if I had been waiting for this opportunity my whole life. Slowly I released all the alienation and anxiety accumulated since junior high school, and sank down beside him as if relaxing into a comfy grave. The hard grit below me rasped and stuck to my sweaty flesh. I was already becoming one with that dark peaceful surface. Deliberately slowing my breath, I stared straight up into deep space.

"God damn it!" Whitey swore, leaning over a barrel to yell into our faces. "Now you're just askin' for it!" Lying on the cool pavement, I wondered how I would first sense death's approach. *Would I feel the growing vibration from the road surface, hear the tires whine in the night air? Would the Hammer leap up, just in time, clearing the center barrier wall to safety like a gazelle?* I hoped so, but I would not. I already decided that, and the finality of my resolve was a comfort.

I saw Whitey's face change from anger to fear. His attention twitched nervously between us and the direction of menace. Then he backed away from the barrel line and disappeared into the darkness. From such a vulnerable position, I found the slightest sounds compelling. Odors, temperature, and distant starlight stood out as each second became precious and memorable. Even that last pungent breath of foul air would seem sweet.

"Get the hell out of traffic, you idiots!" the Bermwalker bellowed. We jumped up and dashed behind the barrel line simultaneously. Moments later a Winnebago with Indiana plates roared by. "Come here Webb, before I fire you." Whitey danced around the Bermwalker and me gleefully as I received my comeuppance. The Bible-thumping rat-fink had probably saved my life.

"You'd better keep an eye on yourself, son," old Joe said, mixing discipline with insight. "Some guys with way too much going on up-stairs can lose themselves out here—and I'll be damned if I'll let you take anybody else with you." The Bermwalker left with Whitey to get everybody coffee. The Hammer eyed me strangely once they left. I pulled ten dollars out of my pocket and offered it to him.

"Take it," I said. "You would have won eventually."

"Don't know 'bout that, Spiderman," he said, taking my money anyway. "When you called my bluff and laid yourself down with me, I near shit my pants. Looked like somethin' strange grabbed hold of you. You were sure-nuff fixin' to die."

I wondered if he was right. *Was I meant to die tonight?* The allure and tension of all the times I had almost grasped death's near proximity returned, and I took up my morbid anticipation again. *If not now, when?*

THE COLLECTION
(The Cleveland Museum of Art)

He was a disease, an infestation from the nether reaches of banking and finance. This rotund pestilence entirely composed of efficiency and small-minded intent. This insufferable Mr. Richard Denison Bunnwad, was our newest board member.

Of course The Cleveland Museum of Art had suffered the attentions of *activist* board members before. Grand Dames of inherited wealth knowing little of art, but a great deal of what they liked. But, as long as they provided the funds to cover the questionable acquisitions they championed, what was the harm in letting them run wild in the auction houses of New York and Europe?

Less innocuous was the great captain of industry using his board position as social decoration, like an honorary degree from a university he never attended. This sort of egotistical popinjay required grandiose projections and five-year plans. Heads needed to roll and edifices required erection to satisfy his appetites. Once again, if he alone provided the largesse to underwrite these obsessions, accommodations would be made. There was always someone in the pecking order ripe for sacrifice, and something suitably ostentatious to cobble together and dedicate in his name.

But when art museum assets were involved, and public donations required, then the scatological reference involving an electric fan predictably came into play. The airing of soiled institutional undergarments quickly ensued. Closets were opened and untold legal and financial skeletons tumbled out. This was not attractive or easily remedied.

Once the checkered past of the industrial titan himself leaked onto the local media, everything went down hill from there. It seems almost impossible to amass obscene amounts of wealth in America these days without taking a fiduciary shortcut or committing a felonious faux pas.

These revelations toppled the commercial colossus in question, which was no skin off our noses. The projects he set in motion however, did not accompany him into lock up. The museum itself was left to pick up the check. Hard enough in any circumstance, but made infinitely more difficult when the collateral damage sent other dodgy patrons running for the hills, lest their own closets be inspected.

Thus the cry went up for adult supervision on the otherwise comatose assemblage of blue bloods making up the board of directors of our fine institution. We needed someone skilled in accounting and compliance; of unquestioned moral fiber and rigid social conduct; a reformer and guardian of the public trust. We needed someone like Mr. Dick D. Bunnwad!

"*Que lastima*," lamented Senora Maria Diaz over her salmon and arugula salad at lunch in the new atrium. "He's asking us to cannibalize the collection."

"*Cannibalize* is such an inappropriate word choice," I argued. "After all, you're not being asked to eat the paintings. Bunnwad simply wants to sell them to pay for...well, all of this." I indicated the rumored-yet-unseen, grandiose, modern renovations surrounding us with a flourish of my plastic fork. "I would rather say *cull*, or possibly...*sacrifice*."

"What difference does it make what we call it?" barked Miss Gronski, the confrontational twenty-something at the table. "It's sacrilege. The damn bankers might as well storm in and tear the exhibits off the walls!"

"Calm yourself, Laura my dear. If the *damn* bankers, as you call them, had not sought cover when this scandal broke, we could easily wheedle the extra funds out of them. As it is, I seriously doubt your photography department will be required to part with anything...significant."

"Screw you, Helmut," she fumed. "Photography is as serious an art form as any in the twentieth century."

"Agreed, but that hardly matters considering the frivolity of all the rest," I teased. "But if you're serious about your suggestive remark, Miss Gronski, you best get to it before I need one of those silly erectile-dysfunction pills to keep up. I'm not getting any younger you know."

"We know," she growled. "All of us working here wonder how you could possibly get any older."

"*Basta*, enough! You two dance together like hungry dogs. We need total unity between all *los departamentos*," Maria declared, mixing her languages with enthusiasm. "Nothing must be sold. *Nada! Comprende,* Doctor Katz?"

"Of course, it's unthinkable," I agreed. "But I don't see why you bring all this brouhaha to me? They aren't going to raid my antiquities department to pay for mere bricks and mortar."

"Why not, Herr Doctor?" taunted Laura, seeking payback for my jabs at her photo fiefdom. "Every one of your moldy old statues would bring millions. He's just warming up with us, before he comes after you!"

The gravity of the situation began to dawn on me. I didn't give a rat's ass how many Italian charcoal drawings or cubist so-called masterpieces went on the auction block. However, the thought of parting with even one of my treasured antiquities grabbed me by the scrotum!

People died to filch these shards of immortal perfection. Aristocratic looters and robber barons toppled whole dynasties to get their hands on this irreplaceable booty. There would never be enough heedless wealth and flagrant disregard for international law to replace them...ever again. Even Nazi villainy had been unable to amass such a trove, employing World War II for cover—but you had to hand it to them for trying.

Something must be done. Since I was the senior department curator at the art museum, responsibility arguably fell on me. "Uneasy lies the head that wears the crown," as Shakespeare wrote. I enlisted Gronski and Diaz to position me strategically around the corner from the director's office. With my age and disability, lying in wait is my sole gambit. My days of hunting down my quarry in the labyrinthine passages of the lower galleries are regrettably long past.

As his tentative footsteps approached, I cut him off with my walking stick. Pinned to the corridor wall like a rare butterfly, he dared not dodge my interrogation.

"Doctor Katz," he mumbled. "I didn't see you waiting there."

"Is something wrong with the lighting, Vincent?" I asked, catching hold of his trembling shoulder in my boney grasp. "I wouldn't notice, you see. Perhaps our finances are so meager the museum can't even replace light bulbs," I joked, displaying the grim amusement of the gaunt and long of tooth.

"No, Doctor, things are...not that bad."

"Then why Mr. Interim Director Maxwell, do I hear rumors from the other curators of plans to sell off the collection?"

"Not selling off...exactly...we simply need to tighten our belts a bit. Rethink our priorities..."

"And what are your priorities, Vincent?" I hissed, crushing him up against the wall so he caught a good look through my dark glasses at the scarred empty sockets beneath.

"Su...su...survival, Helmut. You know how things stand. We need over ninety million for Christ's sake! Look at Detroit. They're threatening to liquidate their entire collection to pay off civil service pensions. Thank God the art museum doesn't actually belong to the City of Cleveland."

"What's all that to me? The collection *is* the museum. Who asked you to build this fancy glass shopping-mall to display it in?"

"I didn't do it," he complained. "All this was the last director's doing. Now that he and his wealthy patron are gone, I must find a way to pay for it...and I will, Helmut, I will. We just need to show the public some...contributions from our side."

"Contributions from my antiquities!" I roared, before the exertion brought on one of my coughing fits. Maxwell used this distress to extricate himself from my grasp and move to where he had a clear path of retreat.

"But they aren't *your* antiquities, are they Doctor Katz? They belong to the museum. Some portion of them must be utilized to sustain us...just like every other asset, in every other department."

"We'll soon see about that!" I coughed out, along with the bloody-tasting spittle recently announcing the approach of my own disappearance.

"Yes we will, Helmut. I'm sending Mr. Bunnwad to speak with you this week. You will cooperate with him...or offer your resignation. Think about it Doctor. It's far better for you to choose the pieces we auction than him. The poor man has no artistic taste at all."

Standing alone in the corridor, convulsed with pain, listening to the retreating steps of authority, I knew what must be done. The colo——o

lection must survive intact. As for anyone who believes the immortal must give way to the expedient, well...I was not so certain.

o——o

Once the phrase, "offer your resignation," hit the grapevine, the over-all mood became less of moral indignation than of character assessment. Certainly one's principles were more easily weighed when measuring in dollars and cents. Would-be revolutionaries fell by the wayside like stragglers on a forced march. They wandered home to their departments and began the sad arithmetic of enumerating what they were willing to loose. Soon it was my turn. By that time, I was well prepared.

"They told me you were going to give me trouble," said the compact meatball of a man invading my office.

"Whatever did *they* mean by that, do you suppose?"

"I don't know," Bunnwad mused. "Maybe they think you're a bit elusive. I had a hell of a time finding your office down here in the basement. Why didn't you move up to the top floor over the atrium with everyone else?"

"Because I have no...attachment to the view," I answered. "I find it easier to work underground, where I'm familiar with the layout," I said, tapping my white and red walking stick for added context. "Sometimes I turn out all the lights down here. I find it much cooler in the dark."

"Yeah, I heard. That must be a blast for your colleagues."

"They learn to adapt...in time. Now let's get down to it, shall we? I'm a busy man. Chop, chop!" I declared, slapping my stick briskly against the metal desk.

"You ever think about getting a fold-up one of those things? It would be more modern and convenient."

"Would it be as sturdy? Would it break when I hit someone?"

"They're not designed for that."

"Then no thank you. Now if there is nothing else...?"

"Only the matter of which sculptural pieces you're willing to contribute to the auction. I need your list this week," he said, in a wry taunting tone. This was evidently the big dramatic moment where I was supposed to fall on my sword and resign. I did not intend to follow his script and had conceived a fairly nuanced scenario of my own.

"And you shall have it," I agreed. "All I require is for you to pick the pieces of your choice. I assume you want the most famous and costly exhibits in our collection? More money gained that way."

"Wait just a minute, Doctor Katz," he gulped. "I'm not choosing. I've got no training for that."

That was the beauty of it, I explained. He was the epitome of the common Clevelander, even if he hailed from the outer suburbs as everyone with money did. If Bunnwad appreciated, or was even marginally aware of any particular work of art, it was certain his lowest compatriots were also.

"The reaction would be huge," I gushed. "Such losses would tear a glaring hole in the heart of the collection. Angry mobs of art students with amazingly visual picket signs would surround the building all summer playing to the media. Ticket sales would plummet! What better way to demonstrate the art museum's commitment to paying its debts?"

"Too much publicity," he shuddered. "We should keep to the second and third rate stuff. Stuff that won't be missed." Now he was on his heels, I began backing him toward the cliff. I concurred with his instincts completely, suggesting we remove only two or three minor pieces from each of the newly completed galleries—to better conceal the losses. He was on board with that, but still resisted choosing himself.

"I'm happy to help you choose," I lied. "While we are at it, I've worked up a rough estimate of the cost of remodeling the new galleries—the time, labor, materials, and collateral costs associated with hiding the damage." My ballpark estimate was purposefully eye opening.

"This is more than we'll make at the auction," he whined. "I can't recommend this."

"They are only *'second and third'* rate pieces," I lamented. "We could select items from the museum workshops—things in the process of being repaired and preserved. I could let you wander through our antiquities storeroom. You can take what you like from there with no remodeling costs involved.

"Now you're talking!" he said.

I find salesmanship akin to snake charming. One must simply maintain eye contact, smile, and bob the head rhythmically up and down to induce an irresistible hypnotic effect.

o———o

"This place is a junkyard," Bunnwad lamented, looking over the worn broken statuary piled against the walls.

"The refuse of all human history," I concurred, rearranging unseen fragments of missing limbs into random positions to hopefully enhance the chaos. "How much do you want, a dozen wheelbarrow loads or so?"

"I wouldn't give a dime for this stuff. What are you trying to pull, Katz? We need stuff collectors will buy. All this may be rare, but it has to be in one piece. I can't auction off rubble."

"Well then, you give me no choice," I reasoned. "We will have to sacrifice from the unseen portion of the collection."

"Unseen by you, or people with actual eyes in their heads?"

"By everyone. This is The Cleveland Museum of Art, Dick. In the distant past, excessive foreign acquisitions and discoveries sometimes turned up items of immense importance and antiquity, which nonetheless could never be considered...art."

"And yet they're still here somewhere."

"Of course, they may not be beautiful, but they are powerful and awe inspiring in other ways. Like the images of Satan and other unnamed demons in our Medieval Gallery, or the fearsome Aztec deities from Mesoamerica that required untold thousands of human sacrifices. They have a masterful repulsion that deserves preservation all the same.

"But are they worth anything?" asked the finance thug, circling the proverbial drain.

"They're priceless in every conceivable meaning of the term," I said, dangling the bait before him.

"Perfect," he crowed. "Now you're talking! Where are they?"

"I keep them safely in the Antediluvian Gallery."

o——o

"The ante-what?" Interim Director Maxwell asked in astonishment.

"The Antediluvian Gallery," said the thoroughly confused Bunnwad. "He said it's where you keep the really ugly art."

o——o

This was not, by the way, anywhere near what I actually said to the perplexed Mr. Bunnwad. But it was what he took away from our conversation. This proved there was absolutely no accounting for his cognition, and he did not give a damn about the sculptures, as long as they sold for oodles of cash. I leave you to decide which characteristic is more odious.

While we're at it, allow me to explain why I was not particularly put off by Mr. Bunnwad's indelicate remark concerning my ocular situation. Without sight, my other faculties have improved considerably. For example, my hearing is quite acute.

Located as I am in this basement where air ducts from all areas of the museum converge, I listen in on *extremely* private goings-on all over the building—once I've located the correct duct. I assure you, I've pinpointed the Director's office duct quite accurately. "Forewarned is forearmed," as they say.

o———o

"There is no Antediluvian Gallery," Maxwell said. "At least I've never heard of one. Helmut is just screwing with you to stall for time."

"He says he's taking me there personally to have my pick of the sculptures on Friday night," Bunnwad said. "I'm meeting him in the atrium at nine p.m."

"That's a First Friday Celebration night," Maxwell said, checking his museum calendar. "You'll be smack in the middle of five hundred drunken yuppies celebrating Halloween. What the hell can he accomplish in the midst of all that?"

"Maybe he doesn't know that. The guy is ancient; maybe he's going senile."

"Herr Katz is as senile as a fox and just as likely rabid. I'm going with you to this *unseen collection*, if only to find out what the old fool has up his sleeve."

o———o

What I did not have up my sleeve were plans to entertain two that evening. That was simply a lucky break. The rest was intentional. The more—the merrier.

First Friday Celebrations were ham-fisted attempts to lure younger fish into the museum's patron net. Apparently, if one trolled for sex and drank heavily among great art, one became an art lover...in time. That was the theory, authored by the same minds draining the endowment fund to build a fish-tank museum mall in the first place. This was part of a campaign branding all of University Circle as a Mecca for upscale intellectual alcoholics, and worked like a charm.

I was standing near the center of the atrium, sipping a passable chardonnay and wearing the required ceremonial robes and head-gear. I could hear the swirl of tipsy costumed humanity around me. It was almost closing time and the hookup frenzy approached a crescendo. Since I no longer belonged to anyone's preferred romantic demographic, I had nothing to fear or hope for.

"What are you supposed to be?" Bunnwad asked, upon finding me.

"A Thugee potentate," I said. "From northern India during the British Raj in the early eighteen hundreds. It's a genuine garment from the suppressed cult. What are you wearing?"

"Our usual clothing, of course," snarled Director Maxwell. "So you did know about the Halloween party. Jesus, Helmut, what was the impetus to do this now?"

"Cover, gentlemen. I can't say I ordered Mr. Bunnwad to come alone, but I am amused he chose you, Vincent to be his chaperone. I'm afraid we will all be required to access unfrequented areas of the property. Normally, that would arouse suspicion. But among our fellow revelers we will be virtually invisible."

"When we visit your *unseen collection*," Maxwell huffed.

"Which doesn't really exist," added Mr. Bunnwad.

"Oh, but it does," I assured them. "Just because something does not appear in the museum's catalog, doesn't mean it is not in our treasured possession."

"A whole gallery, hidden, undocumented, forbidden to display, and known only to you. That's pretty hard to swallow, Helmut," Maxwell said. "Even from a crazy old spook like you."

"This isn't the first time the museum's suffered major remodeling," I reminded them. "There are foundations layered atop basements and buried under cellars galore. You will discover no lack of dead forgotten spaces to fill."

I loathed giving them the whole song and dance, but I needed something to string them along. The party was breaking up and the confusion of mass exodus and clean up was to our advantage. I enlisted Maxwell and Bunnwad to steer me clear of the costumed melee, through the center of the old 1916 building, and out the south doors.

The night was mild for October. We moved down behind *The Thinker* statue, explosively enhanced by radical art critics in the sixties, to avoid prying eyes from inside the building. I gave out a long shrill whistle, much to the alarm of my companions, and waited. Vaarg came up out of the darkened museum lagoon and sat beside me.

"What the hell is that?" Maxwell shuddered.

"My service dog," I said, taking hold of his dripping leash. "Come along, he'll lead us to the entrance."

"It looks like it has scales," Bunnwad observed.

"Vaarg is a very rare breed," I confided, as we marched down the steps and around the raised south patio. Vaarg plunged into the tangle of ornamental bushes and trees bringing us eventually to the metal access door hidden from view. I released his leash and he vanished into the darkness with a piercing howl.

"This looks like a maintenance door," Maxwell observed. "What makes you think there's anything behind it besides electrical boxes and sprinkler lines?"

"How do we get in?" asked Bunnwad.

"We wait to be invited," I answered. "You may find what's inside disturbing. Most truly ancient sculpture represents Gods and demons. They're used as conduits between entity and supplicant to beg favors or avert calamities. It has been said that *'God created man in his own image'*, but I'm afraid the truth is quite the opposite. Man created his Gods to resemble himself."

"What about the Egyptian deities?" Maxwell argued. "How does your theory explain the Minotaur, Sphinx, or Babylonian lions with human faces?"

"They're conceptual hybrids of human and animal attributes— nature spirits anthropomorphized for our acceptance," I explained. "What you will see in here will not resemble those. The Gods in here will appear almost entirely alien."

"Why is that?" asked Bunnwad.

"Because they are not our Gods."

With that, an ominous scraping of rusty levers and stubborn gears emanated from behind the metal door and it opened out toward us. Maxwell and Bunnwad jerked me back defensively with them as a squat frog-ish figure stepped out—dressed outlandishly with luminous moon-like eyes and scaly braided strands of hair cascading from his wide misshapen head.

"Good God!" Maxwell shouted, uncertain whether to flee or fight.

"Steady gentlemen! This is only Uthul Vaarg, my servant," I reassured them. "From your reactions I imagine his Halloween costume is quite effective. I've asked him to prepare the Gallery for us."

"He's a Vaarg too?" Bunnwad said. "How's that work?"

"Where he is from, and where the rites of these antediluvian cults survive, pets are...part of the family," I explained, accepting the torch and loaded offering basket Uthul Vaarg provided, and stepping carefully down into the darkness.

o———o

Once clear of the door, I lit the torch with a cigarette lighter so
Maxwell and Bunnwad could follow. They crept down the mossy
stairs (which I navigated by memory) like timid thunderstruck bump-
kins to stand beside me.

"I can't believe all this was just below our feet," Maxwell admitted.
"I feel like a tomb raider."

"No electricity then?" Bunnwad said.

"Nothing modern must remain here," I instructed. "Only bedrock,
fire, and dripping ooze suit the elemental nature of the pieces displayed." The metal door slammed shut. My companions gasped and
ran back up to it, straining together in fruitless struggle against the
unyielding mechanism.

"Gentlemen, please calm yourselves! Uthul Vaarg will see to the
door," I said. "We must not be disturbed from above. Certainly the *two*
of you have nothing to fear from an old blind man like me! Come along
now, I'll give you the grand tour." Maxwell and Bunnwad managed to
compose themselves at my chiding and we descended the long staircase while I narrated the highlights of the fetid downward shaft from
memory.

"These are the twilight entities, the bridge between the old ages
and our own. Here we have Baal, the God of the Philistines who lost
domination to Jehovah. This is Moloch. Notice the scorched furnace-
like belly cavity. Newborn infants were cremated alive in there to
curry favor. And this is the prehistoric fish God, Dagon, sacred to the
ancient aquatic races."

"They don't seem that unsightly," Maxwell observed. "I thought
you said the exhibits down here were...more horrific." We reached the

bottom of the shaft that ended in a large chamber. It contained a dark stagnant pool surrounded by six rough-hewn caves tunneling back away from the torch's dim flickering light.

"They're transitional forms, semi-grotesques as it were. The pieces you have come to see reside in those caves. Here Maxwell, take the torch. I have no need of it. You two may explore at your own pace while I prepare for the offerings."

"You're conducting some sort of ceremony for them?" Maxwell said.

"I must. These are primitive deities, Vincent. They do not understand nor abide the effete practices of artistic appreciation or mere tourism."

"Sounds like a lot of hocus-pocus to me," Bunnwad said. "But go ahead anyway. This ancient mumbo-jumbo is your department, Doctor Katz."

Indeed it was. It had not been easy to contain this aspect of the collection. Sacrificing my own eyesight to defeat their previous guardian had been an early cost. Yet there were significant benefits. My guests set off to explore the six caves of dominion as I knelt beside the pool of eternity in solemn supplication. While their anguished cries of disgust and revulsion echoed in my ears, I began the liturgy of surrender.

"Oh God, Helmut," Maxwell confessed, upon returning. "They're worse than I could ever have imagined. No wonder they can't be shown! Just gazing on them is physically terrifying, even...nauseating."

"I threw up all over myself," reported Bunnwad.

"Yes, the workmanship is truly evocative of their grotesque natures," I agreed. "Devotion and adoration played no part in these cults. It's essentially all fear and loathing."

"Sounds sickening. When can we get out of here?" Maxwell

chaffed.

"Have you made your choices?" I asked.

"What's to choose, they're all hideous?"

"Nevertheless, you must each choose at least one entity. That is why I brought you here and the benefits from your selections will be considerable."

"I don't see how," Maxwell said. "But to end this disgusting tour, I'll pick the big elephantine thing with the wings and face full of tentacles."

"Great Cthulhu, an excellent choice." I lifted the copper, offering basket, intoned the chant of transference, and placed it carefully in the shallow pool. I knew a greenish effervescence would begin to bubble and swirl in and around it.

"What's in the basket?" Bunnwad asked.

"Rocks, broken pieces of colored glass, and shards of clay pottery," I answered. "That which is precious and beautiful to us, becomes worthless and vile to them, and vice versa. Which entity have you chosen, Mr. Bunnwad?"

"None of them. Who needs those kinds of nightmares?"

"I'm afraid we can't finish here until you do. Choose the least objectionable."

"All right, already. Jesus Helmut, if I knew I had to do shit like this, I would never have become a board member."

"That would have been easier for all of us, Dick. Now choose one!"

"I'll take the goat-like thing with all the eyes. Maybe someone could use it in a haunted house business."

"Ah, Shub-Niggurath, the immortal bitch of the forest and mother to a thousand young. Interesting choice, I would have figured you for a Yog-Sothoth man." Now that the second choice had been made, I coughed up a bloody infected offering into the pool from my conveniently diseased lungs. That done, I removed my dark glasses, cupped my hand in the viscous fluid, and brought some up to my lips. The taste was sharp and sulfurous. I applied the remainder to my face and eye sockets. Perhaps I should have bathed myself entirely, but time was short. The summoning had begun.

I retrieved the offering basket, stood up, donned my glasses, and took the torch back from Maxwell. Moving to the opposite side of the now seething pool (and thus closer to the stairs), I addressed the shaken duo.

"Now you have seen the Elder Gods of this planet and chosen among them. Likewise, they have seen you and accept your preferences. I, who cannot see or therefore be seen, leave you to them." I threw the torch into the bubbling water, plunging the gallery into absolute blackness. Maxwell and Bunnwad's terrified shouts and confused curses chased me up the stairs (I had practiced climbing many times before), to the metal door. My shrill whistle signaled Uthul Vaarg to allow my escape and seal the door behind me.

The transformed gold, silver, and precious stones filling the offering basket in return for our first sacrifice, no doubt glistened in the moonlight, causing my servant to jibber excitedly. The anonymous donation of this extremely valuable trove would go far toward satisfying the museum's creditors and keeping the collection intact.

I felt the benefits of my second sacrifice by improved breathing and the first sensations of nascent ocular regeneration. In the cool night air, I contemplated many more decades of devoted service to the collection. For a short time, piteous screams of terror and pain mingled with the slop and slither of ectoplasmic tentacles and the gnashing of stony teeth echoing hideously from within.

SLAG
(The Cuyahoga Valley Steel Mills)

It looked like Hell. Not the ancient medieval vision described in Dante's *Inferno*, but an industrialized clockwork version bent on manufacturing filth and damnation. Despite this fearsome appearance, Juan's father and generations of hard-working Clevelanders living on its boundaries and employed within its ashen bowels, knew it simply as the steel mills.

As a young child, Juan got the grand tour of this reeking valley of devastation by merely crossing the high spindly ironwork of the Clark Avenue Bridge. There he could be almost eye to eye with the roaring flames emitted from its vent stacks and glimpse the seething cauldrons below amid swirling clouds of steam and sulfurous fumes. It was always a fearful crossing as the bridge was high, long, and narrow—strung together of rusty soot-encrusted trusses insubstantially balanced on a few crumbling concrete pylons.

If you made it across from West to East you arrived in the monochrome neighborhoods along Pershing Avenue. Most of the cheap clapboard housing here was supposed to be painted white. Instead everything was tinged a reddish brown—coated in layers of the mills' toxic exhaust. The dominant winds in Cleveland blow from the Northwest, so the eastern edge of the industry-clogged Cuyahoga River Valley chokes on the worst of its airborne filth. The river itself and Lake Erie beyond swallow the effluent remainder.

This is where Juan grew up. And this is where he vowed never to return. He thought even the army was preferable to a life in the mills. But, after tromping through years of arid stony deserts and mud-walled compounds stinking of shit and death, he thought again.

It was not a homecoming. His mother and father were dead and the house they never owned, torn down and replaced by a junkyard. Clark Avenue Bridge was missing also, demolished before Juan reached puberty. But Pershing Avenue remained, brutally amputated and uselessly jutting out over the dark vista of mills that still memorialized the phantom bridge by the severed stumps of its concrete pylons.

o———o

"It's only temporary," Juan reasoned. "Until I can afford to go full time at Cleveland State."

"Yeah whatever," Tony, his old high school buddy said, between too many bottles of cheap beer. "Your timin' is good. They're hirin' a shitload of guys to start up mothballed number three mill. Drop your old man's name. The union will grandfather you in."

Getting in hadn't been that easy in decades. During WWII and the 50s, they couldn't find enough bodies to feed these mills. They yanked whole villages from overseas, build cheap housing to cage them, and boiled the ethnic melting pot with heat from molten steel.

But the decades since had seen a greased downward slide toward extinction. Unlike Pittsburgh, where dead steel mills turned into parkland as their economy evolved, Cleveland refused to let go. These mills might be polluting industrial dinosaurs—but they were our Goddamned dinosaurs, and we loved to hate them.

"You're lucky," the union rep said. "They've done nothin' but lay guys off and shutter mills since you was in diapers. These new owners are all Gung-Ho. The old union guys are all retired or dead like your pop—so there's a few openin's."

The "new" owners were from India. That's not Indiana; it's *India*—turbans, the Taj Mahal, and fat idols with elephant heads. Cleveland corporations couldn't even sell out to Europeans anymore. We had to beg for scraps from the third world.

"It's a small world after all," the union rep sang with sad irony from the theme song of a Disneyland ride. *"It's a small, small, fuckin' world. You start on Monday."*

o———o

That first day was a Chinese fire drill inside the administration building: paperwork, aptitude tests, physical exams, and a graphic safety film designed to weed out the squeamish. Everything that went on in the mills could kill you, most in horrible ways at thousands of degrees Fahrenheit. Juan witnessed lots of messy death in the army— so he was somewhat immune to this horror show. You can't ignore the visceral reality of death when you've gathered up the scattered pieces of your buddy in a plastic bag. After the film, the suits in charge handed out protective gear and told everybody where to report the next day.

The first weeks were a hazing process, cycling through all the toughest jobs available. Management quickly found out who wanted to work and who just wanted to get paid. Recruits also acclimated to the rain of derision thrown at fresh meat by foremen, supervisors, and veteran workers. Most were deviant sexual or ethnic slurs, but one stood out below the others. If they really hated you, they called you "Slag."

"It's the worthless shit they throw away," Tony told him. "The nasty poisonous stuff that bubbles out of the steel and gets burned off or discarded." All over the apocalyptic landscape of the valley mills there were gray steaming mountains of it.

As part of the orientation, management dragged Juan and the other recruits through all its industrial stations-of-the-cross. The unloading docks on the Cuyahoga, where conical mountains of brown taconite, white limestone, and black coal awaited consumption. The monstrous reeking coke ovens, where coal baked until it became something even more volatile. The obsidian-hued blast furnaces, squatting like gigantic machine idols, as conveyor belts fed raw materials into their hellish fiery bellies to be melted and shat out into turd-shaped railroad cars as molten iron. But iron, however free of waste products and impurities, was just the first step.

The next step happened in the oxygen furnaces, where super-heated molten iron was coaxed with infusions of scrap steel and exotic minerals into transforming itself as steel. Molten steel, in turn, poured into the hungry maws of immense continuous-casters inhabiting the cavernous metal sheds running for miles along the Cuyahoga. These shaped the cooling malleable steel into a myriad of useful forms serving any purpose. Then came the finishing sheds, where steel was cold rolled, galvanized, or electro-plated to taste. Finally, the warehouse docks held finished products awaiting delivery within site of the vast steaming waste piles, where mammoth earthmovers plowed through the scrap and slag endlessly.

Every machine, building, or process involved was enormous on a cyclopean scale. Ever-more superlative conceptions of size were essential for a finished product solely measured in tons. In this land of gigantism, the human forms resembled those of insects or even bacteria infesting titanic environments.

"Crush you like an ant, zap you like a fly, or toast you like a marshmallow," were the warnings veteran worker, Grady used to describe each dangerous job to his young charges. "Plenty o' ways to die here boys—try not to pick one."

Juan had difficulty working up much interest in Grady's repetitive warnings. Once you've faced down jihadist crazies armed with AK47's and RPG's it's hard to focus on inanimate menace. Instead he scrutinized the gray-haired foreign supervisor who watched them closely day after day. He always wore the same safety gear all workers needed, but he wore it in a pristine academic manner. Clearly he was not there to get dirty. When the workers broke for lunch, Juan approached the silent older man by reading his name badge—A. S. Gupta, Ph.D.

"Doctor Gupta," he said, "how do you like Cleveland?" There was no response as the supervisor continued to focus on his clipboard. Juan didn't know if he was being ignored or if the good doctor wore the rubber earplugs Juan preferred to skip. He gave it another shot. "Pretty different from India, I suppose."

"Quite different," the aloof supervisor said, without looking up from his writing. "I have not returned there in many years. I was last in South America."

"Does your company own steel mills there also?"

"Of course," he said, finally raising his gaze to meet Juan's. "North America is not the only place we are expanding."

"Are their mills as run down as ours?" Juan asked. Gupta took a long moment to answer. Juan felt he was contemplating more than the question asked.

"On the whole, I feel both will benefit from our investment. However Mr. Guzman, as you are the first of your colleagues to engage me, perhaps we should continue this conversation in my office after your shift ends." Juan recognized the polite variation of *"get back to work"* and postponed his curiosity until he was off the clock.

o———o

Gupta's office was not on the top floor, indicating mid-level status at best. He wasn't even listed on the corporate executive flow-chart in the lobby of the administration building. He occupied a respectable corner office offering maximum visibility over the mothballed number three mill.

Juan cleaned himself up a bit, washing his hands and face, but did not change clothes to avoid being a complete suck-up. He stopped to knock even though the door stood already open.

"Come in Mr. Guzman. Take a seat. I will be with you shortly." Gupta was busy behind his desk, but Juan was too nervous to plop into the only other chair. Instead, he kept to the center of the room, surveying the decor with casual interest. The first thing he noticed was a modest altar in one corner complete with incense burner, paper flowers, and the aforementioned elephant-headed deity.

"Hey," Juan said, as casually as his curiosity allowed. "You don't see one of these in every business office."

"Possibly not," Gupta said, "but I assure you they are quite common among businessmen in my country. That is Ganesh, remover of obstacles. I believe we have many obstacles to overcome at mill number three. Don't you agree, Mr. Guzman?"

"I guess so. But I'd prefer you call me Juan. Mr. Guzman was my dad."

"We all have to grow up and assume these roles eventually," Gupta said. "According to our records your father and mother have passed away."

"Yeah, three years ago last month. Car accident."

"Allow me to express our condolences. I see you are unmarried, with no children or close relatives, having spent some time in the armed forces."

Juan was unprepared to be researched. He must have deserved it by talking to Gupta. Juan half expected to be *thanked for his service,* which would feel weird since he hadn't actually served this guy. He did expect a perfunctory handshake, but received neither.

"So Mr. Guzman, how does it feel to be in your father's old position?"

"A little weird. A lot has changed since I left—like your new management. I never even realized India had a steel industry."

"That is not surprising. Americans show little understanding of other countries. Anticipating such ignorance, I have something to show you." Gupta spun a large book around on his desk, opened to an illustration of some monument. "This is a photograph of The Iron Pillar of Delhi. It is approximately twenty-three feet high, twelve inches in diameter, and weights seven tons. It consists of a single casting of flawless iron formulated to never rust—even in the hot wet climate of India. It was manufactured almost a thousand years before the birth of your Christ."

"Wow," Juan said, with a little hint of disbelief. "That's pretty damn old."

"Yes," Gupta said. "In fact, it is possible that iron and steel making was invented in ancient India. The advanced metallurgy of today is directly descended from eastern alchemy—the mythic quest to turn lead into gold."

"If you say so."

"I do, and therefore it is not as *weird* as you Americans seem to think for a corporation from India to own a steel mill half a world away...in Cleveland."

"I never said it was," Juan backpedaled. "I just always thought modern steel making was our thing."

"*Modern* steel making, as you refer to it, is fundamentally the result of two dominant aspects of western culture—greed and impatience."

"Well, maybe," Juan said, with a little laugh at how contentious this conversation had turned. "But we call that profit and efficiency."

"Yes, you do," Gupta said, closing the book. "Good day, Mr. Guzman."

o———o

"What a prick," Tony said, at the bar where he and Juan tried getting lucky with girls drinking under age. "He's new, some kind of specialist in restartin' old crap mills. He'll disappear when number three goes on line. Good riddance to foreign garbage—am I right?"

"I don't know," Juan replied. "He beats brain-dead sergeants barking orders."

"He's a *fuckin' tourist*, Juan. Come see our dyin' city! Make millions! Screw the dumb-shit locals!" Tony yelled over the jukebox music. "I'd love to push that towel-head under a movin' rail car! Now drink up *dude*, you're fallin' way too far behind."

o———o

Old number three was an obsolete mess, but not completely a lost cause. If a steel mill could be seen as a man-made volcano, *mothballing* made it a dormant volcano—still alive, but sleeping under a protective crust of neglect and inactivity. If you *shut it down,* cutting off the heat, power, and lubrication, then the residual liquid metal and slag in the machinery seizes up and welds the whole shebang into useless post-industrial sculpture. That volcano goes extinct.

Extinct steel mills become scrap metal or ironic sites for lesser things like shopping malls—like the new *Steelyard Commons* mall across the river. Some call it *"Fly Ash Flats"* for the toxic residue buried under its big box stores and parking lots.

"In many ways, we are fortunate," Doctor Gupta said, standing God-like in front of a phalanx of company and union bigwigs high on the catwalk of number three's oxygen furnace. "This mill was equipped with technology incompatible with today's high-volume production. Therefore, it is perfectly suited to the small-batch artisan steel we intend to produce here in Cleveland."

Juan, Tony, and the rest of the new and veteran workers chosen for the project stood below on the cluttered mill floor, straining to make sense of Gupta's words echoing around the immense metal building.

"The challenges are great," Gupta continued with dignified yet dramatic gestures. "But, together we will meet them. Every piece of this mill must be inspected, cleaned, repaired, or replaced before production can begin. I have scheduled the inaugural run of the *new* number three mill precisely five months from today."

After the perfunctory applause, but before the other big shots had their say, Juan turned to Tony for reassurance. "Only five months? Look at this place. Do you think we can do this?"

"Who cares," Tony said. "We get paid by the hour."

"That's a shitty attitude," said Juan. "I think it's exciting, like beginning a special mission."

"Ever go on 'special missions' over there in the sandbox, Mr. Hero?"

"Sure, I've been on my share."

"How'd that work out for you?"

"I'm still here."

"Yeah, you're right here beside me," Tony hissed. "takin' orders and suckin' hind tit from this *fuckin' third-world slag*! How damned excitin' is that?"

Their mission hit the ground running the very same day. The newer workers were assigned to various crews under veteran workers. Juan was with Grady, and Tony was assigned to O'Donnell. Juan was fine with this because Tony's attitude made any job harder. Gupta knew his business and their earlier interaction, however contentious, seemed to lay the groundwork for some trust. Gupta used Juan's group for the more important tasks, and Grady's experience plus

Juan's enthusiasm usually got things done right and on time.

Not that there weren't problems. The reconditioning process seemed to require working on every machine from the inside out. The dangers of crawling around inside aged machines led to numerous accidents. Nothing much beyond smashed fingers, minor lacerations, and first degree burns, but number three mill's X-days-without-accident billboard never reached double digits.

The pace and difficulty of their work had something to do with it, but Gupta's ingenious short cuts added to the potential danger. It was like a continuous live-ammo exercise, and Juan could feel a *friendly fire* incident coming on. Gupta never showed any emotion or remorse when something went wrong. Although first aid and emergency procedures were always applied, the pace of work never slowed. Finally, Juan felt he had to go over Grady's head and alert the union.

○——○

"I see," said the union rep, when Juan met him at the union hall. "So, are you accusin' this supervisor of recklessness? 'Cause that would be some serious shit."

"No, I'm just worried things will get worse," Juan said.

"Well to clarify your situation, take a gander at this report we've put together on the company's operations. Remember, this stuff is only between you and me, comprende?" Juan paged through the report covering the international company statistics over the preceding few years.

"Wow," Juan said. "They're everywhere."

"Yeah, they're floodin' the zone. They buy into any country that allows it, use that toehold to pry open the door for their imports, flood the market, drive down prices, bankrupt competition, then raise prices again once everyone else is gone.

"Does that work? Can they keep making money doing that?"

"Yes and no," the union rep said. "If you're spread around the world wide enough, you can lose in one country for a long time while makin' it up somewhere else. Smaller companies can't fight you everywhere, so one by one they crap out. It's sort of a cancer strategy. But that's not what I wanted to show you. Look at these numbers."

"That's a pretty high accident rate," Juan said.

"These ain't accidents...in the third world lost fingers don't even count."

"This is a death rate?" Juan said, in horror. "They can't do that here in America can they? I mean OSHA and workman's comp would be all over their ass. There would be fines and lawsuits."

"You're right, absolutely," the union rep agreed. "That's why they carry monster insurance and retain an army of lawyers and lobbyists. Look kid, you can fight this if you want—be my guest. But Cleveland needs these jobs, and so does our union. I'm just sayin' you'll lose, and it's gonna be lonely in the trenches."

"Jesus Christ!" said Juan.

"Maybe he'll help," said the rep. "Go to church. Light a few candles like your mother did. Otherwise, I'd watch my back, look out for my friends, and bank some fat paychecks."

o———o

As the clock ticked down the tasks got harder. Machinery too small to crawl into but too heavy to lift, even with the massive overhead cranes in the mill, still had to be reconditioned. Disassembly took too long, so Gupta got creative. They'd lift one side at a time. The floor would support half the titanic weight, but workers still had to crawl underneath the other side to complete the work. "I'm not going under there," Juan said. "No way in hell I'm doing that."

"Somebody got to," Grady said. "Look here, son, I'm skinnier than you. I'll go under, you keep hold o' my boots. Yank me out quick if shit goes wrong." Juan deferred to experience, although it broke every safety code ever written. They pulled it off all along the left side of the roller arrays just fine. But on the right side, Juan heard the tiny explosive *pings* of cable strands snapping and pulled Grady out with all his might.

The roller array came down with a deafening crash as the murderous cable whipped up like a broken rubber band, tangling itself around the overhead crane, barely missing its operator cage. Juan and Grady survived, but Grady's trailing arm was crushed and had to be amputated on site.

o———o

Later on in the hospital, Juan was startled by the victim's jubilant mood. "Here's our hero," Grady said, to the crowd of relatives clustered around his bed. "Saved me from Old Slag himself."

"Not all of you," Juan replied. "I blame Gupta, we shouldn't have tried that."

"What's done is done. Slag got my arm and I got early retirement and disability pay. Old Slag wanted to swallow me whole, but he only got one bite."

"That had nothing to do with slag, Grady. That was rusty steel in the cable."

"What you know 'bout it, soldier boy? You got it all backwards. Slag ain't no bad shit pulled out o' steel. Steel is what we takes *from* Old Slag. Iron, limestone, coal, and all the other good stuff we grabs out o' the earth—it all belongs to Old Slag. And he expects payment for it!"

o———o

Gupta, Grady, Juan, and the crane operator all got written up for safety violations. Against the union's wishes, Juan filed a grievance against Gupta and the company for ordering the work. Before it even came up for a hearing, Gupta promoted Juan to Grady's old position as crew chief. "You've got to be kidding," Juan said to Gupta afterward.

"Why, Mr. Guzman? Your actions were heroic, and you have always exhibited extraordinary commitment to our project."

"But not to the way you're doing it."

"Then find a better way, Mr. Guzman. We face grave resistance, but I see nothing in your record to indicate you cannot overcome adversity," Gupta said, in cold rational tones still holding some whiff of taunting. "Your grievance against me must run its course, but so must our work on the mill."

They made a strange team. Gupta set the tasks and Juan figured how best to accomplish them. Some union guys, including Tony and O'Donnell, complained about this breech of seniority, but Gupta continued to confer with Juan despite formal job title or pay scale. The work progressed and the X-days-without-accident totals actually climbed into double digits—until a serious electrical accident sent several more workers to the hospital.

o——o

"Sabotage?" Juan said, up in Gupta's office as the good doctor gazed out over the nearly renovated mill. "Who would do that?"

"You tell me," said Gupta. "Someone wants us to miss the completion date, desiring it intensely enough to injure our employees."

"Well, I don't think it's the union. They want the mill to open. We've stepped on a few toes, but not enough to get people hurt."

"But, enough for some people to strongly desire continuing to be employed," murmured the Doctor.

"I don't follow you," said Juan.

"Number three mill will employ a sizeable number of workers

during production, but not as many as it has during renovation," said Gupta. "Some people must be laid off once we are successful." This revelation worried Juan along with all the suspicion, prejudice, and superstition he'd encountered since starting at the mill. What was going wrong here?

Out in the desert it became abundantly clear he and his fellow countrymen didn't belong. No amount of heroism, camaraderie, or sacrifice could ever put things right. Intervention unleashed ancient terrible forces they could not understand or control. But here in his own country, in his hometown, he still could not fully understand or identify the enemy. Even worse, just as overseas he didn't know who to trust or what they really hoped to accomplish.

o——o

Two weeks later their backs were up against Gupta's deadline. The sabotage attempts were foiled by nonunion rent-a-cops. It was the night shift. Iron ingots had been packed into the oxygen furnace. Gupta and his metallurgy chefs were cooking up their first batch of specialty steel. They swarmed around the control room dressed like goggled alien surgeons pressing buttons amid glowing dials and gauges.

As the oxygen furnace began to glow an ominous red-orange, workers took their positions dressed in the reflective insulated moon-suits designed to protect them from the withering heat produced—at least temporarily. The random sparks and sputters of boiling steel could be endured with little danger, but longer contact with a hot glob of liquid metal would still cook the flesh inside.

Ominous shadows of these bulky golems moved back and forth on the walls armed with long needle-like spears. These were the metal control and sampling rods used to manipulate machinery and metal too hot to touch. Like the proverbial "ten-foot poles" folks wouldn't use to even touch disgusting or dangerous things, these primitive tools defined the minimum proximity of safe approach.

Now the finished liquid steel poured into the giant open crucible. The white florescent illumination was tinged with the dangerous sulfur yellow and cherry red of glowing metal. Higher and higher the overhead crane lifted the full crucible on its dangerous arc to the waiting feed-trough high atop the floodlit caster. Fiery sparks and sputters cascaded down along the mill floor like burning rain.

Juan and Tony waited up on the catwalk of the continuous caster. Their hand signals guided the crane operator as he suspended the crucible directly over the trough. Juan climbed up the metal ladder attached at his end of the trough and reached out with his control rod. He hooked its end to the glowing trapdoor at the bottom of the crucible and pulled. Slowly it slid open and a golden stream of blister-ing-hot steel began to fill the trough. Juan climbed back down to his station on the catwalk.

Tony kept his distance on the other end of the trough as an on-going Niagara of glowing sparks cascaded down between them. Disguised by silver hoods, dark safety glasses, and face shields, they could barely recognize each other or hear their shouted communica-tions.

"It's fillin' up too fast!" Tony shouted. "There must be a blockage in the trough somewhere!" Juan looked down through the open grid flooring of the catwalk and could see no emerging tongue of steel extruding out onto the water-cooled rollers below.

"Give it time," Juan yelled back. "Shut the trap door a little and let the caster catch up." Tony climbed the ladder on his side of the trough and hooked his control rod to the trapdoor. He appeared to pull with great effort, but the door didn't budge.

"I can't close it!" he screamed. "It's goin' to overflow!" Overfilling the trough would cause a molten wave of metal to cascade down the front of the caster ruining most of the renovation and probably killing them both.

"Pull harder!" Juan yelled. "I'll climb up and push from this side to help!"

"Screw you!" Tony yelled back, already abandoning his post. He pushed his emergency button on the way down. Howling sirens and flashing emergency lights erupted inside the mammoth metal shed. The workers below scattered for shelter outside the building. Even the crane operator panicked, abandoning his cage to scramble away from his perilous overhead position.

Juan knew he should run as fast as his bulky suit and thick insulated boots would allow. He also knew five long months of hard work was minutes away from destruction. He'd been in this situation before—the life or death decision.

Americans could approach such a situation still believing in their own indestructible super-hero luck, as delusional as that was. But their adversaries, with ten pounds of high explosives strapped to their bodies, had no such illusions. They had something else—something Juan had never experienced, but still respected.

Glancing toward the control room, Juan saw a figure still watching through the thick glass windows after all others had fled. Juan could not see who it was, but something passed between them—a shared compulsion deciding everything yet to come.

Juan climbed his side of the trough again. To close the trapdoor from this side he would have to balance out on the trough as the molten steel crept up toward the edge, hook the door, and push. Push hard enough that, even if the door closed, he might still loose his balance and fall into or off of the trough. Either way was probably certain death, but Juan preferred breaking his neck on the mill floor to swimming in the three-thousand-degree soup.

Balanced as well as possible, he hooked the door and pushed. Expecting it to be stuck or partially fused, he almost fell when it slid easily. Tony had faked it, which meant he was a lying saboteur among other things. The liquid metal flow slacked off and Juan looked down to see a thick ribbon of formed steel now flowing out of the caster and onto the rollers below. He adjusted the door opening to match the decreasing surface level in the trough and climbed down. Before he could turn around and cross over to shut off the emergency alarms, a hard blow stunned Juan between his shoulder blades. He dropped his control rod and fell to his knees trying to shield his head from repeated pounding. "What the hell?" he shouted, seeing Tony attacking him with a control rod.

"Eat shit and die, traitor!" Tony screamed. "I'm sick of your slag-lovin' ass!" Murderous as his intentions were, Tony never was as tough as he thought. His street fighting was no match for Juan's military training. Juan grabbed the end of Tony's control rod on the second attempt to crush his skull and used Tony's reactionary pullback to regain footing. Then Juan suddenly reversed his pull on the rod to push, knocking Tony's hood and face shield off. The falling sparks burned into Tony's scalp and face. He let go of the rod to cover his head with gloved hands. Juan flipped the rod around to knock Tony's feet out from under him.

Rolling defensively away on the scalding hot catwalk, Tony slipped under the railing and fell off the edge. He caught himself and hung there screaming for help. Juan could have saved him, pulled him back on the catwalk, or possibly been dragged down himself. Instead, Juan let Old Slag take the bastard.

Tony's gloved hands could not keep hold of the hot steel-spattered catwalk as his fingers began to cook. He slid down the front of the scalding caster with a wailing cry and landed face first on the extruding red-hot steel. He stuck immediately. Sizzling like a hamburger patty, he was drawn under the crushing water-cooled rollers that flattened and spread the moving steel for hundreds of feet, before it was chopped by powerful hydraulic shears into manageable-sized slabs.

o——o

Because no witness ever came forward to dispute Juan's benign version of events on the catwalk, Juan and Tony were hailed as hero and martyr. Both were also written up for not heeding the emergency warning. Juan became a pallbearer for Tony's nearly empty coffin, because his family could never recover much of him from the flat hardened steel. Being one of the last hired, union seniority rules required Juan to be among those laid off when the new number three mill went into production. Gupta probably could have found him a toehold in management, but Juan decided to take his earnings and start college instead.

o——o

"Maybe I'll study engineering or business management like you," Juan told Doctor Gupta before he left.

"My doctorate is in religious studies," Gupta said. "My family's financial interests are responsible for my position here. However, I also will be leaving. I am starting a new facility restoration in Ireland. Before we part, I have a gift for you, Mr. Guzman." Gupta handed Juan a richly carved teakwood box. Inside was the idol of the elephant-headed god and the incense burner. "Perhaps there will be obstacles to overcome at your university also."

"Thanks, it can't be much different than my mom's candle lighting," Juan said. Glancing toward the modest corner altar, Juan found it now occupied by a black many-armed goddess brandishing a sword and a severed head while dancing on a corpse. A wicked-looking knife and a glass bowl partially filled with dried blood accompanied it.

"This is Kali, the goddess of death and the destroyer of enemies," Gupta said, caressing the idol with one ominously bandaged hand. "She requires sacrifices of a different sort."

SMALL BUSINESS

(Buckeye Road—The West Side Market—The Cleveland Flea)

The customer arrived as night fell. He knocked twice on the back door as he'd been instructed. An overhead light snapped on and a viewing slit opened. Two cold blue eyes stared out.

"What word you choose?" asked a young female voice with an eastern European accent.

"Ah...dra, dra, Dracula," stuttered the nervous young man. The piercing blue eyes rolled partially back in disdain.

"Is stupid word." The slit closed, the light snapped out, latches and deadbolts were turned inside, and the door opened inward releasing a sliver of sickly yellow light. A small white hand with sharp blue fingernails extended out, seductively found a grip on the buckle of the young man's belt, and yanked him inside with surprising strength.

He was roughly shoved against a metal pillar. His hands were pulled painfully back around it and shackled together. A petite teenager with blue eyes and flowing mane of golden curls shoved the barrel of a small revolver up under his chin.

"Dra..., dra..., Dracula," he gasped in fear.

"What, already?" teased a statuesque older brunette wearing scanty black leather and heels. "These are the introductions, darling," she purred, moving quickly from behind where she shackled him to slam the door and reengage the numerous locks and deadbolts. "You must learn to save your safe word," she advised, searching him intimately for weapons and valuables, "until it's absolutely necessary. Otherwise we'll never have any fun," she warned, simultaneously kissing his face and squeezing his testicles painfully.

"It's just, this... ah... neighborhood see... see... seems kind of dangerous," he explained.

"What did you expect...Disneyland?" Magda replied, removing the prearranged fee from his wallet.

"No Mickey Mouse, only rats," hissed Rina, rubbing the barrel of her loaded weapon playfully over his groin.

o———o

Magda loaded the metal trays of meat onto the cart in the refrigerated basement of the West Side Market. Rina waited in silence, her cold blue eyes catching every movement and lingering on the fresh red and white mottled sausage.

"You might help me, you know," Magda complained, wiping her hands on her bloodstained apron. At forty years old, Magda felt the cold and damp seeping into her joints. She kept up her appearance and was proud of her figure and dark Hungarian tresses. Yet age was taking its toll; a little consideration from her much younger blond partner would be appreciated.

"You load, I push," Rina answered with calculated brevity.

That was perfectly telling of their relationship, Magda thought; a partnership so cut-and-dried, favors traded, duties divided, a fair exchange of goods for services. Magda hoped for much more—hungered for it through the long tense silences haunting them even while entwined in each other's arms. Whatever human warmth and caring had existed inside her little playmate went missing now. It was stolen, burned away, or sold off piece by piece early on. This was not poor little Ekaterina's fault—it was her fate.

As Rina pushed the heavy handcart down the wet corridors of the basement toward the freight elevator, Magda marveled at her hidden strength and determination. If one edge of the unwieldy cart should catch against the old wooden bumpers lining the cement walls, she would tug and struggle with it like a longshoreman. If Magda tried to help, Rina would stomp her little rubber boots in the bloody slop underfoot, cross her arms in a defiant pose, and refuse to go on. Their iron bargain must be maintained. Weakness and pity were not tolerated where Rina came from.

Magda loaded, Rina pushed. Magda rode up with the cart in the elevator while Rina hosed the blood and loose scraps of meat off the floor and down the drains. Yet upstairs in the bustling ethnic melting pot of the West Side Market, Magda was the undisputed queen of her family's venerated butcher stall and sweet Ekaterina played the silent golden princess at her side.

Magda arranged the display cases, schmoozed the customers, and made the sales. Rina cut and weighed the fresh meat, wrapping each order tightly in stiff white paper bound with knotted string. Precious Ekaterina was the lovely blue-eyed bait drawing hopeful men from other stalls, repeat customers, and casual tourists like bees to honey. Magda, ever the gregarious hostess and flirt, parlayed their interest into cash, leaving customers happily supplied with her delicious Magyar sausages and meatballs, but otherwise unsatisfied.

o——o

The West Side Market opened on Mondays, Wednesdays, Fridays, and Saturdays. Most of the days and nights in between were for preparation and restocking. Sundays were traditionally a day of rest. In Magda's parents' and grandparents' time that meant church and family. For her and Ekaterina, it meant local craft shows and street fairs. There was no rest for the wicked—or for small business owners hustling to stay afloat in Cleveland.

They carved out a thriving niche market in fetish jewelry and leather goods. Typically they sold to the Goth crowd and the romantic vampire wannabes. Lately the local steam and cyber punk movements were also burgeoning.

Once again their roles were carefully delineated. Magda made the jewelry from leather, bone, and recycled bits of antique jewelry and timepieces. For the cyber punkers, she incorporated chunks of cell phones and other personal electronics.

Ekaterina did the leatherwork. Apparently she learned the craft back in the old country—wherever that was. She spoke Russian of course, but that didn't nail anything down. Russians were all over Eastern Europe and the Balkans before being cast adrift by Glasnost and Gorbachev. The somewhat luckier ones made it back to the imploding motherland. The rest drowned in rising tides of rebellious nationalism.

Sometime after the Berlin Wall fell, the USSR fragmented, and communism collapsed, little Ekaterina was bartered off to the sex trade. She grew up as a perverse commodity. She experienced the not-so-invisible hands of the marketplace intimately. To survive her harrowing childhood, Ekaterina created a second persona to shield her fragile soul from the many atrocities conspiring to shape and nurture Rina. This same Rina, escaped naked and bloody one night into the mean streets of New York City, where Magda rescued her, after a fashion.

At first, the discovery of Ekaterina felt like kismet. Later Magda would come to learn the full price of Rina's desires and her own. Still, they had each other. Love, revenge, and dependency made a potent brew. Symbiosis took hold. One thing led to another and then too much worse. A partnership formed as all their pieces fit together by sheer necessity. Now they were a finely tuned machine. Perhaps not unstoppable—Magda knew the devil lurked somewhere in the details—but formidable nonetheless.

In the open air of the street fairs each could be at their best. Ekaterina worked the dyed skins with her strong little hands—silent, meticulous, and adorable. Magda performed in her element as a queen of commerce—talking up the customers, closing sales, and scouting for those particular customers with unfulfilled forbidden needs making them likely prospects.

○———○

"Crawl like worm!" Rina barked, whipping vigorously with her feathered lash. Her foreign accent was perfect for this. Magda was fascinated watching her work up to the "happy ending" her raw experience and obsessions demanded.

The customers loved it. She was just the right mixture of sexy, disturbing, angelic, and vicious. Magda led them around the ceramic-tiled abattoir in her family's basement on a leather leash, while her bare-breasted partner, decked out in thigh-high boots and minuscule leather G-string, supplied the erotic punishments their customers desired and deserved. The old meat hooks and chain hoists hanging from the ceiling added to the ambiance, and the central butcher's table—with its butcher-block surface, recessed drainage channels, and improvised restraints—completed the dungeon-like setting.

Magda's parents, grandparents, and uncles could not have imagined what went on in their basement workplace now. That didn't matter. Their unhealthy vices and artery-clogging diets killed them off years ago. Once Magda confessed why there would be no husband for her and no grandchildren for them, they despaired of passing the business and traditions on to the next generation.

Yet Magda continued to surprise them. Her dedication to *Csonka's Magyar Meats* was everything they could have hoped for from a son-in-law or grandson, so they went to their graves content. When Uncle

Drago finally passed on the secret family recipe from his deathbed—the house, business, and heritage became hers.

It was not an easy legacy. Hired help proved larcenous and unreliable. Her Hungarian Buckeye Road neighborhood deteriorated and changed ethnicity. Magda grew fearful of living alone in the family home, although she needed its basement meat-processing facilities to continue the business.

Rent at the West Side Market doubled. Magda feared losing the family butcher stall, passed down since 1912. She escaped from her financial worries on a drunken weekend with girlfriends in New York City. That's where she rescued Ekaterina—or perhaps Rina captured her.

Like past refugees, Rina brought new energy and skills. She urged Magda to branch out into erotic services and fetish handicrafts. More importantly, she possessed the appetite to recreate the ancient family specialty that revived their market stall and made it unique again.

The price for this was steep, but Magda was willing to pay. Magda loved and needed Ekaterina in her life. But to hold onto Ekaterina, Magda had to satisfy Rina, and Rina drove hard bargains. They swore a Russian mafia blood-oath to each other making normal business contracts and even Russian Orthodox marriage seem like child's play.

"Up pig dog, up!" Rina commanded, slapping the customer's naked buttocks.

Magda led him roughly to the table where he eagerly stretched himself out across the rough surface. This guy had angry tribal tattoos covering his body. Magda hated that. A tasteful decoration on an arm or chest was manly, but the current fad had taken things way too far. She felt men were becoming a gender of satanic sideshow freaks.

"Tie pig dog for punishment." Rina growled, mere inches from his face. He acquiesced gladly, focusing on her taut nipples and gleeful expression with misplaced enthusiasm while Magda began to bind him.

o——o

Magda took a break on the balcony overlooking the main market hall. She could sneak a few puffs on her French clove cigarettes up here, although smoking had been banned in all municipal buildings for years.

"I need to pee," she told Rina, who grunted acceptance of this customary falsehood. Ekaterina spoke enough broken English to handle most transactions herself, even if she preferred to remain mute and smile demurely while pointing at the appropriate price tag or posted credit policy in reply.

Up here Magda could focus on the big picture. Overlooking the crowded landscape of their retail world, she could ponder its meaning and their place in it. What she couldn't envision was a clear way forward, an acceptable end game for herself and her demanding little Czarina.

What she did see was trouble approaching. It was sashaying officiously down the center aisle toward their stall in the person of Savannah, an acquaintance from the bars as well as the Health Department inspector assigned to the market. Magda stubbed out her acceptable vice and stashed it back in the Altoids tin hidden in her apron pocket. She raced down the stairwell to disarm the approaching confrontation.

"Hello princess, you ditch that ol' wicked witch you shack up with?" Savannah asked.

"Magda, not here," Rina answered, crossing her arms defiantly.

"I can see that, honey," the sassy inspector quipped. "What I don't see is why a fine young thing like you stays with that nasty ol' bag of bones. You should find yourself a classy new mama, someone who won't make you work like a dog all the time. Someone to give you all the pretty things you deserve. Someone like me."

"Rich black mama—like you," Rina scoffed.

"That's right, ain't nothing wrong with that," Savannah bragged, looking around casually for eavesdroppers before advancing through the gap in the defensive rectangle of display cases. "You should give me a try. Everybody knows dark meat is tastier than white," she said, closing in on her quarry.

"Meat is meat," Rina said, lowering her gaze toward the butcher knife lying next to the meat scales.

"I bet all you got to eat is sausage. I bet they fed lots and lots of those nasty sausages to you over in that commie hell-hole you came from."

"She came from New York City," Magda said, slipping past Savannah just in time to discretely move the knife away from Rina's grasp. "What are you inspecting today, Savannah darling?"

"I'm inspectin' any damn thing I want, Magda. That's my job," sassed the inspector. "I should be closing down this smelly ol' pork stall of yours, right now. What do you Hunkies put in this stuff anyway? It always smells kinda funky."

"Is big secret," teased Ekaterina, allowing Rina's scowl to slide into her own mischievous smile.

"An old family recipe," corrected Magda pleasantly. "Would you like a free sample? You should try it, darling. I'm sure you've never tasted sausage like ours."

"Oh, I had my share of sausage, Magda. You can be sure of that. A fine woman like me can get all the *sausage* she needs, but I prefer cheesecake, as you know."

"As do we," agreed Magda. "But too much cheesecake is bad for the figure—as you know, Savannah darling."

"My figure is fine!" Savannah fumed. "You're the one could use some more damn paddin' Magda—you ol' skinny bag of bones! Ain't I right, princess?"

"Fat disgust me," Rina declared, spitting on the floor in brazen Slavic insult.

"I could fine her for that! Spittin' ain't allowed in here. There's no cause for her to be disrespectin' me like that."

"Forgive her," Magda purred, ushering the feisty inspector out from behind their display cases and back into the aisle. "She was only defending her friend. I'm sure you didn't mean to insult me Savannah darling, especially while you're on the job. I'd have to report that to city hall if you did."

"Eat cheesy cake," Rina hissed. "Go there!" she finished, pointing toward the *Antonelli Bakery* stall down the aisle.

"This ain't over," said the inspector to Magda as she moved away. "I'll be seein' y'all in the bars."

"Not if we see you first, darling."

o——o

The next Sunday found them at the Cleveland Flea Market, held in a parking lot on the third weekend of every month. It was a sunny cheerful day and interest in their wares was high. Ekaterina and Magda worked happily with each other. Worry was the last thing on their minds, until Savannah hunted them down and waved it in front of their faces.

"Why are you doing this?" Magda asked.

"Because I can, bitch," Savannah crowed. "These legal papers give me the power to test every scrap of meat y'all got at the market. If I find any funny stuff in that meat, even one damn rat turd—and I will, I promise you—I shut y'all down and raid that rat's nest of yours on Buckeye where you make it. What you think of that, Magda...darling?"

"I think there must be some arrangement we can make."

"Oh there is, honey," Savannah laughed. "There most certainly is. Y'all can loose your grip on that little princess of yours and tell her to step out with me."

"What if she refuses?" Magda said, knowing cold blue eyes watched their negotiations.

"We both know who calls the shots in your house. Anyway, she ain't no spring daisy. Folks I know on Buckeye see your customers come and go—most of them anyway. I know all about your dirty little side business, even if you don't advertise in the porno pages of *Scene Magazine.*"

Magda considered Savannah's threat. The financial hit they would take was the least serious consideration, although it was probably the only one Savannah knew she was wielding. Then there was Ekaterina to consider, what she had suffered already and how Rina would react to anything more. Finally there was the recipe, handed down through ages of famine, war, and deprivation—the brutal, hungry times when pork was scarce, but death was abundant—the secret of her family's survival. All this fell on Magda's shoulders now to protect or destroy. "We'll need some time to talk it over," Magda said.

"Y'all got time, honey. Tomorrow, I can tear these papers up and enjoy that child's company—or I can tear up your business. Y'all choose," Savannah said, as she sashayed away blowing smug kisses at the stone-faced Rina.

Magda turned to her beloved Ekaterina. "Did you hear?" Magda said softly.

"I hear," Rina said, her cold eyes searching Magda's face for any hint of betrayal.

"What do you think?" Magda asked. "We'll handle this any way you want—I swear it."

"I think...no problem. I see black mama...one time."

"Thank you, thank you," Magda said, kneeling down before her and kissing her hands in subservience and gratitude. "I'll tell Savannah tomorrow."

"No," Rina said, yanking her hands away from the distasteful feel of tender emotion. "Tonight. Tell black mama now."

"Where will you meet her?"

"Midnight, at market."

"Do you think that's wise Ekaterina darling? You could do it in the bars, or at our house where we would have more control."

"I take control," Rina said, disgusted by Magda's fears. "Give keys for market basement."

o——o

Once the restraints were cinched down tight, Magda had to move quickly. Rina's excitement could not be contained for long. She slapped, whipped, and swore at the customer with a building frenzy.

Of course, there was his prearranged safe word—not that most decided to use it. After all, they paid handsomely to be abused and humiliated. It amused Magda how easy it was to recruit customers once she suggested little virginal Ekaterina would be their tormentor. The local Goth community virtually crawled with socially awkward males eager for her intimate mistreatment.

Magda stripped off her black leather bustier and short skirt to straddle the customer's chest, strapped his head down, and forced the rubber-ball gag into his mouth. This kept his thrashing and vocalization to a minimum and gave her a privileged view of his reaction. "Here it comes," she whispered, licking his ear delicately. "Are you ready, darling?"

Meanwhile, Rina began to expertly manipulate his manhood with her hand and mouth while carefully retrieving the razor-sharp blade hidden in her boot.

As the customer climaxed, spraying them both with his seed, Rina deftly slit the arteries in his groin. Blood gushed out, pumped in great spurts by his orgasmic heartbeat, flooded the table, filled the drainage channels, and poured off into Rina's cupped little hands. She smeared it ecstatically over her face, hair, and body, howling with animal hatred, washing away her psychotic rage at all men with hot liquid revenge. Magda watched carefully as the customer's ecstasy transitioned through pleasure to pain and eventual peace. It didn't take long for them to bleed out. His heartbeat, so frenzied at first— slowed to a stop against her naked loins.

After castration, gutting, and dismemberment, his carcass was ratcheted up to drain. Then Ekaterina and Magda retired to a warm shower together to rinse off their befouled bodies, sharing in the passionate climax of Rina's vengeance. When all their lusts were slaked, they held each other and kissed tenderly—just as they had that first night in New York City when Magda discovered the blood covering Ekaterina's perfect nubile body came from someone else.

Having shared the intimate ritual that cemented their complex relationship, they dressed, donning butcher's aprons to begin the real work. It took hours for the two of them to fully process the entire carcass. They utilized every part and possession even grinding the skeleton and teeth into bone meal, then hosed the spilled and splattered offal down the basement drain. It was a long night's work and

Csonka's Magyar Meats opened for business at 7 a.m.

o——o

The morning after the Flea Market and Rina's tryst with Savannah, Cleveland awoke to a dreadful catastrophe. Four months shy of the West Side Market's one-hundredth anniversary a mysterious electrical fire blackened the interior of the building overnight.

The basic structure, being totally constructed of concrete, brick, and ceramic tile was still intact, but the merchant's stalls and inventory were ruined by soot, smoke, and water. Because of electrical failure and the heat of the fire, all the meat stored in the market's basement coolers could no longer be sold and was ordered destroyed by incineration.

City hall vowed to rehabilitate and reopen the historic structure in time for the centennial. All the vendors' rents were suspended until the reopening and emergency low interest loans were arranged for anyone with insufficient insurance to cover their losses.

No one was injured by the fire. Amid all the chaos and confusion after the event the unexplained disappearance of a single troublesome health inspector vexed authorities. Her whereabouts were never discovered, but her rumored inappropriate activities in the building that night with an unknown juvenile did suggest illegal behavior and possible culpability in the suspected arson. That said, without any further evidence, she was eventually forgotten and replaced.

o——o

For Ekaterina and Magda the four months off from the market felt like an extended honeymoon. They suspended their erotic service business until the market stall would need restocking and concentrated on their fetish crafts enterprise.

With all the days of the week open to selling their wares, they traveled to craft shows and art fairs all over the state. Magda was happy and content in a way she had never been before. With Savannah absent they could return to the nightlife of the bars, where their size, age, and hair color duality played quite well and made Magda the envy of her peers. Ekaterina enrolled in an English as a second language course and developed new interests more typical of the young lady she had become. They looked into her applying for citizenship, but her lack of birth or immigration documents made that impossible. Magda considered adopting her, but Rina found the symbolic reversal of power...intolerable.

Their personal finances also experienced a significant improvement. Ekaterina's new style of supple undyed leather goods...decorated with angry tribal tattoos, sold very well indeed.

MOUNT PLEASANT RANGERS

(The Mount Pleasant Neighborhood)

"The Bugman's got Di'vonte's sister!" yelled Little Marco from the cracked weedy sidewalk in front of Auntie's house on Rexford Avenue. Tyrone's crew of junior high schoolers were chilling on her porch because it was stinking hot; his Auntie's house was on the shady side of the street, and nowhere they were welcome had air conditioning.

"Where's he at?" Tyrone said, jumping over the front porch railing with Dwayne and the Harris twins, Nate and Ali close behind.

"Jasmine says he took her down a cellar o' that rat-hole 'partment on 116th and Craven." They all knew where Marco meant. There were lots of boarded-up and burnt-out apartment buildings in the neighborhood, but the abandoned "Parkside Gardens" was the nastiest. Nate and Ali took off running with Dwayne lagging behind because he was both the fat and muscle of the crew. Little Marco began to follow, but Tyrone waved him off with another assignment.

"Hustle up to the Arab's deli and have him call the cops."

"They been called," whined Little Marco. "I wanna see ya'll beat his ass!"

"Do as I say or I'll beat your ass," Tyrone threatened before he ran after his friends. He was glad somebody already called 911. He would be even happier if the baby wanna-be thugs, like Little Marco kept out of it.

The Bugman was an old wino who used to scratch out a living by fumigating neighborhood houses for roaches and bedbugs. But his addiction got the better of him. Now he was homeless, sleeping rough in abandoned buildings with other crack-heads, junkies, and whores haunting Mount Pleasant streets.

By the time the crew arrived, a small group of old women had gathered across the street, wringing their hands and moaning prayers to Jesus for mercy and deliverance. Their grown men were absent as usual, being previously engaged at work, sleeping off drug and alcohol binges, or doing time in any number of correctional institutions.

Tyrone and crew were about to rush the building when several squad cars pulled up and the cops took over. They didn't take long to flush out the ragged population hidden inside. The cops had been there before for much the same reasons and knew they would be there again on many sad instances to come.

They dragged the Bugman off in a squad car. Di'vonte's little sister, Lestina was treated at the Cleveland Clinic and returned to her mother's family relatively unharmed. Nothing more was said about this until Di'vonte turned up two weeks later. He had been in juvenile detention, caught standing lookout for his big brother's drug dealing. Since his brother was over eighteen and serving more serious time, Di'vonte was now unemployed and hanging with Tyrone.

"How's Lestina doin'?" asked Tyrone.

"She got scratched up and all," Di'vonte said. "But she'll deal with it."

"Did he do things to her?" asked Nate, hoping for juicy details.

"What you think, numb-nuts?" growled Di'vonte. "Sewer rats don't grab kids like her to play jump-rope!" Di'vonte gave a hard-ass stare to the rest of the crew, warning off further indecent questions about his sister's ordeal. He possessed dangerous street credibility now, having quit school and done time. "Anyway," he said. "Bugman didn't take anythin' off her she won't be givin' away soon enough. Our old man won't let nobody press charges 'cause he likely done worse to her his own self." Nobody commented on this shameful statement. They'd all suffered through family dramas sadly lacking in moral restraint.

"What we aughtta do," Di'vonte hissed, from the seething well of anger filling up inside. "Is clean out Shit-Hole Gardens for good."

The abandoned apartment building was boarded up by the Cleveland Housing Department after the Bugman's crime like after every serious incident before. But already some of the plywood was torn off and a familiar plague of undesirables reoccupied the property.

"This part of town be zombie-fied!" proclaimed Di'vonte. "We gotta snuff that shit out."

"What you mean zombiefied?" asked Nate.

"I mean they's all zombies!" railed Di'vonte. "Dead folk what won't lay down an stay dead. You seen'em, like on movies and TV."

"They's drunks and crack-heads mostly," said Ali. "An' some crazy mothers what can't pay fo' they pills."

"What's the difference ya'll?" argued Di'vonte. "Alkies, crack-heads, junkies, and crazy ho's full o' crabs and clap—they all wanna die or they would sure-nuff get off that shit. They's good as dead already. They's nothing but walkin' dead folk, and *walkin' dead* be zombies!"

Tyrone and crew considered Di'vonte's revelation. In a way it addressed fears they all had about the destructive behavior of their elders—a fate they worried might be contagious or inevitable for themselves. If these folks were monsters, not relatives and neighbors requiring sympathy and forgiveness, then the dismal questions of who, how, and why hanging over their own lives got much easier. After all, every kid knew what must be done to monsters...and zombies.

"So..." Tyrone asked, after the weight of Di'vonte's theory settled in upon the assembled boys. "What you mean by snuff?"

The young street-Svengali just smiled, placed a finger gun to Tyrone's head, and mimed pulling its trigger. Tyrone knew what that meant, and his former crew also understood their shift in leadership.

There was just one snag left to sort out.

"Whatta 'bout the cops?" asked Dwayne, who was never one to say a word until the more talkative crew members whittled down any issue to its finest point.

"Whatta 'bout'em?" answered Di'vonte with a wicked grin. "They ain't never done nothin' but snatch zombies up, stew'em in the slammer, and dump'em back here on us. Cops ain't gonna give a damn when that ends...or fret 'bout who had the 'nads to finish it."

The crew spent the rest of the week with their new leader Di'vonte, watching zombie movies at Auntie's house, studying the best techniques for a clean kill. Everybody agreed it was useless to target anything but their heads. Still, a lively discussion ensued on the best tools for the job and where they could steal them.

The choice of a name for their new posse also took up a good deal of time and became contentious. Various devilish titles were advanced, but met stiff opposition from Tyrone who stressed the "protective" nature of their enterprise. Finally, the Harris twins' devotion to the TV show, *Walker, Texas Ranger* and tendency to vote together triumphed. They dropped the western association, added their neighborhood, and the Mount Pleasant Rangers were born.

Once suitable weapons were stolen, like a sturdy barbeque fork, brass fireplace poker, and baseball bats they modified with long spikes the crew broke into a gas station after hours to use its electric grinder.

"What you gonna use?" asked Nate, as Di'vonte lounged around watching sparks fly as the others sharpened their arsenal to lethal perfection.

"Never you mind," Di'vonte sneered. "I got a secret weapon, and I'm gonna steal a can o' gas while we is here."

"What for?" Tyrone asked, never quite sure of their new leader's true intentions.

"What anybody need gas for?" he answered. "To burn shit."

After gaining the necessary weapons and followers, their budding urban Napoleon needed an attack plan. Di'vonte divvied up the next few days among his troops to scope out the numbers of their enemy and when best to strike. He even enlisted Little Marco and his elementary-school cohort to spy on the Gardens from their nearby classroom windows and playground, while the older boys stood night time surveillance.

During daylight, the ruined apartment building was quiet, as the addicts and whores slept off their mostly nocturnal endeavors. Evenings they were out breaking into cars and turning tricks to feed their fatal ravenous habits. But early mornings between three a.m. and the sickly creep of dawn they were all back inside, drunk or stoned and ripe for the picking.

The Rangers all lived in Auntie's house, because she worked double evening shifts at nearby nursing homes and slept most days. She was off on Sundays, spending them at bible study and church services. With two or more run-down storefront churches at nearly every major intersection, the beleaguered population of Mount Pleasant was ritually divided into those who prayed, and those who preyed upon them.

Tyrone's Auntie put up with the boys because she was maternal and evangelical to a fault. She knew their single mothers and absent fathers were far too busy entertaining their own demons to care about the little devils she sheltered.

For their part, Tyrone, Di'vonte, and the rest of the Rangers did Auntie's shopping, housework, and lawn maintenance. They pretended to go to school, fear God, love Jesus, and live up to her trust. It was a cozy domestic situation as long as nobody paid attention to the details. Mount Pleasant was not a community that dared scrutinize itself too deeply, being morbidly fearful of what it would discover.

About four a.m. Saturday morning the Rangers snuck down Rexford Avenue through back yards and vacant trash-strewn lots toward their objective. They kept their distance from houses with dogs that might raise an alarm, hiding their weapons in an old duffle bag. Di'vonte used Dwayne as their pack mule, loading him up with both the bag and full gas can.

Outside the Gardens, hidden in the shadows cast by dim illumination from the few still-functional streetlights, they armed themselves and spread into a two-pronged attack. There were two places where the homeless squatters tore down the plywood barricades for access. Dwayne and Tyrone slipped in the front way through a missing porch window and Di'vonte and the twins threaded themselves under the crumbling rear fire escape and down through a cellar door.

Inside, the city's sun-baked heat lingered, steaming up the odors of festering mold and rotting garbage. Feeble light from distant streetlights barely penetrated through splintered window frames and missing brickwork. Tyrone switched on his stolen flashlight and guided Dwayne through empty apartments and stifling hallways searching for the zombies' nest.

Di'vonte bet the zombies would stay low on the first floor or in the basement because the apartment's roof was full of holes and leakage would render the upper floorboards into a maze of rotted pitfalls and booby traps.

He was right. In a basement furnace room on a floor covered in fetid mattresses, the Rangers found the nest. Ten reeking bodies snored and coughed in fitful slumber as the Rangers closed in from opposite doorways. Their flashlight beams flitted from body to body like voyeuristic fireflies, landing on a toothless mouth, a tangled mop of hair, an exposed sagging breast.

For a moment, most of them felt a tug of pity and the urge to leave such hopeless squalor well enough alone. Then Di'vonte kicked the nearest bodies and two ragged sodden creatures stirred to life.

"Who you?" growled an old whiskered junkie, shielding his bleary eyes from their focused beams. "Leave us be, we ain't got nothin'." The second figure struggled into a kneeling position on the spongy mattress flooring.

"Got money boys?" she babbled through swollen lips caked in old lipstick. "Blow ya'll for a twenty." Tyrone swallowed queasy doubts he dared not share with the others. *Zombies don't talk,* he thought. *Zombies don't suck cock neither.*

Di'vonte smiled at the pathetic harlot, drew his brother's Glock pistol from his waistband, and blew a large hole through her face. "Well," he said to his Rangers, as the zombie herd awoke from the deafening blast. "What ya'll waitin' for?"

Dwayne pushed past Tyrone and began braining helpless bodies along one side of the room with his spiky baseball bat. The twins attacked the other side, beating and stabbing like frenzied demons with their bat and fire poker. Tyrone stood paralyzed by the scene before him. The bobbing flashlight beams danced from gleeful Ranger faces to crushed skulls and punctured eye sockets. Then Di'vonte caught Tyrone in a glare of accusatory light.

"What's up?" Di'vonte taunted. "You with us or not?"

Tyrone was afraid to answer, afraid of losing face, afraid of Auntie's all-seeing Jesus, afraid of Di'vonte's gun. Without warning a rag-covered figure rose up beside Tyrone and pushed him away from the door where he stood transfixed. The zombie escaped into the darkness and up a stairway to the first floor.

"No witnesses, Tyrone!" yelled Di'vonte. "You a Ranger, remember?" Tyrone knew he was right. Not about the zombies, but about the consequences of discovery. There was no going back for any of them now.

The zombie disappeared amid the maze-like blackness of empty rooms. Stalking the sound of panicked footsteps, Tyrone thrust his flashlight beam into the darkness like a Jedi light saber. Abruptly the footsteps stopped. The zombie went into hiding somewhere in the rooms ahead. His footprints in the dust led Tyrone ever closer. The zombie's heavy breathing should have betrayed him, but Tyrone could not hear it over his own labored breath and pounding heartbeat.

The desperate zombie burst out of a closet door and tackled Tyrone, slamming him to the dusty floor. Tyrone thrust the barbeque fork deep into his attacker's thigh, but the zombie grabbed him by the throat. The flashlight rolled into a corner and threw a cone of light on the zombie's face.

It was the Bugman. Di'vonte was right. The cops had given up, letting these animals loose to haunt his neighborhood over and over. Tyrone jabbed the Bugman again and again, felt his weapon penetrate what should be vital organs, but still the undying derelict squeezed him in a death grip.

As Tyrone began to loose consciousness, a vicious baseball swing exploded the Bugman's cranium, spattering the floor and Tyrone's face with pieces of scalp and brain. "You gotta go fo' they head, Bro," said Dwayne, helping him off the floor. "You shouldda known that."

Dwayne and Tyrone dragged the Bugman's body down to the mattresses where Ali was dousing everything with gasoline. The Rangers went out the cellar door and Di'vonte tossed a match back inside. By the time the fire trucks arrived, the Rangers were all cleaned up, eating milk and Cheerios for breakfast as Auntie arrived home from work.

Of course, the "Mount Pleasant Massacre" made the news. But the grisly charred remains caused far less concern than anyone, including the naive Rangers, imagined. Even the bulk of the Parkside Gardens survived, as the brick and concrete of the basement room provided less than ideal tinder for successful arson.

Cleveland had far bigger problems. Rival drug gangs were in the midst of an all-out turf war. Collateral damage amid the innocent was rampant. Children as young as five months died in hails of gunfire meant for fathers or older siblings. The drive-by shooting became epidemic.

The overwhelmed police contributed their own excesses. They gunned down kids playing with toy weapons and riddled one defenseless couple with enough firepower to rival the movie carnage of *Bonnie & Clyde*.

In truth, much of the city and certainly the Rangers' neighborhood was an evil three-ring circus of gangs, scandals, and ponzi schemes. These entangled government, business, and even well-dressed preachers promising eternal afterlife salvation while draining neighborhood resources in the here and now. Amid all this the misguided vigilantism of the Mount Pleasant Rangers was a gruesome sideshow.

"I told you," Di'vonte said. "Nobody give a shit 'bout zombies."

"They ain't zombies," said Tyrone. "Just crazy poor folk, worse off then us."

"Nobody give a crap 'bout them neither." Di'vonte decided.

Tyrone hoped success at Parkside Gardens would end Di'vonte's obsession with zombies. Instead the Rangers expanded their "Zone of Protection" from Martin Luther King Boulevard to the Kinsman/Union triangle. There were over fifty possible zombie nesting sites within the zone. Catching zombies at any one site was difficult, but checking every place each night was impossible.

"We gotta narrow the odds," said Di'vonte, launching "Operation Firebug." They burned a house each night for two solid weeks. Three held nests. Live zombies burned just as crispy as the dead ones at Parkside Gardens.

Tyrone had nightmares about Auntie's house burning with Rangers asleep inside, so he was glad Di'vonte showed up pissed-off one afternoon. "I been visitin' lock-up," he said. "My brother says we bein' stupid 'bout that zombie shit."

"How so?" asked Tyrone.

"What's in it fo' us?" asked Di'vonte. "My brother says, 'What's in it fo' us?'"

"Protection," said Tyrone. "We's standin' up for our hood."

"Bullshit!" Di'vonte fumed, reliving his brother's disdain. "He talkin' cash, fool! Perks fo' me an you. Forget them stupid mo-fo's, Dwayne, Nate, and Ali."

"He ain't wrong," said Tyrone, hoping they could forget zombies and do something more reasonable, like stealing cars.

"Yeah," said Di'vonte. "But that will change. I got some ideas."

Di'vonte had his eye on a younger crack whore named Shawna. She worked the corner of Oakfield Avenue and 126th, turning tricks in a boarded- up storefront. The Rangers caught her at dusk and dragged her back inside. Each took his turn in her, even Tyrone. For most it was their first time, but none would say so.

"Why do me like that?" Shawna complained. "You is young bucks,

I'd do ya'll half price." But they had no money and Di'vonte wasn't nearly done. He blew a nasty hole in the middle of her forehead, just as he finished inside her. The other boys stood around for a stunned moment with their pants around their knees, then zipped up and burned the storefront down around her body.

Tyrone started attending the Second Tabernacle Missionary Baptist Church with his Auntie on Sundays. He prayed to forget Shawna's lifeless girlish face, which he now remembered from when she used to babysit him in childhood.

But no amount of prayer could help the Rangers. Now they waylaid zombies before returning to their nests, stealing the booze, drugs, and sex earnings that enslaved them. The zombies died and burned just the same, but with alcohol, drugs, and cash the Rangers became rowdy and neglected their household duties. Auntie kicked everyone out but her nephew, Tyrone.

The Rangers settled into an abandoned house on Ely Avenue near Luke Easter Park where they could wash up at the neighborhood recreation center. Their zombie pickings grew scarce as fear and the homeless grapevine finally cleared the neighborhood of all but its most brain-dead addicts.

Di'vonte hired Little Marco and his network of grade-schoolers to find new victims. Rangers now burned houses owned by mortgage cheats cashing in on fire insurance. They were all on a greased slide to Hell, and Tyrone knew it.

"I wanna quit," said Tyrone, to a bleary-eyed Di'vonte nodding out on a filthy couch reclaimed from garbage day on a tree lawn.

"No can do, bro," slurred Di'vonte.

"How come?" asked Tyrone.

"'Cause the only way you stop bein' a Ranger," said Dwayne,

smashing his spiky bat into a wall to demonstrate. "Is the same way you stop bein' a zombie."

"You got it, bro?" taunted Di'vonte from his drug haze.

"Yeah," said Tyrone, backing out the splinted doorway of their squalid new headquarters. "I'll catch ya'll later."

"Catch us tonight 'bout sunset," ordered Di'vonte.

"Where at?" asked Tyrone.

"Someplace you'll feel at home," Di'vonte teased. "Little Marco says a new bunch o' zombies is squatin' in the Parkside Gardens."

Walking through his neighborhood with a "zombie fork" hidden under his fall jacket, Tyrone thought about his terrible summer. Starting as Auntie's best boy, he became defender of the hood, then a murderer, arsonist, and now a rapist. He wanted to change again before winter. He would use this night to leave the neighborhood forever or get rid of Di'vonte, redeeming himself and his crew.

Tyrone met the Rangers across the street from the battered hulk of the Gardens. The plywood was torn off every door and window by the firemen. The result looked full of holes like dozens of dark dead eyes. You could get in or out from any direction, making their plan of surrounding the zombies difficult.

Di'vonte split them up, each Ranger entering the building alone, planning to chase whoever they found into a central kill zone. The glimmer of twilight and the open windows changed the look inside. It's haunted emptiness and the echoing creek and groan of doors and floorboards spooked the Rangers as they stalked through the maze of rooms and passages. Eventually they converged on the blackened furnace room and its crater of burnt-out ceiling reaching the first floor.

No zombies were found. Instead Tyrone, Nate, and Ali looked down from the first floor as Dwayne and Di'vonte discovered a clean sheet of paper on the scorched basement floor below. On it was a simple request, scrawled in red crayon with the shaky block printing of the young or nearly illiterate.

"It says, 'LOOK OUTSIDE'," Di'vonte said. Tyrone moved to a nearby window, open to the street they just left, and saw a chilling sight. Twenty or more zombies stood in the gathering darkness armed with killing tools much like their own. As if his appearance at the window was a signal, they began to advance.

"There's a damn army o' zombies out here!" yelled Nate, from a window on the opposite side of the building.

"Here too!" screamed Ali, from the missing front door.

"Get outta the basement!" Tyrone shouted down to the Rangers below. "We's surrounded by zombies!" The duo in the basement scrambled for the same stairway used by the Bugman to escape upstairs as the furnace room filled with a mob of snarling murderous zombies. Di'vonte shot two of them as he and Dwayne made it to the first floor. Tyrone and the twins were beating and stabbing dozens of ragged frenzied attackers as they tried to force their way through first floor windows and doors, but there were far too many openings to defend.

"Run to the top floor!" commanded Di'vonte. "There's only one way up 'cause the fire escape's fallin' apart." The Rangers retreated all the way to the fourth floor, as the entire building filled with every wino, crack-head, junkie, and whore from fifty blocks around, all armed to the teeth and wild for revenge.

The Rangers made their stand on the top landing, pushing filthy bleeding bodies back down the stairs upon those climbing up from below. Di'vonte shot three more, which pooled the rest momentarily out of range into loud, seething mobs in the hall and rooms below. "How much ammo you bring?" asked Tyrone.

"One clip," mumbled Di'vonte, shaking with the fear of defeat. "But I don't know how many I used."

"I heard five shots," said Nate.

"You got maybe seven left to get us out," figured Ali.

"Not near enough," decided Dwayne.

"Some suckers will crawl up the back way any minute," Di'vonte whined. "We gotta find a way out."

"We can jump," said Nate.

"Four floors up?" said Ali. " We might as well use them bullets on our self."

"There's a big old tree upside the building," remembered Tyrone. "We can 'scape down that before they knows we gone." The Rangers hurried down the center hall as quietly as possible over the warped damp flooring. In a nearly roofless apartment they saw the dark shape of the tree just outside a window. Dwayne, Nate, and Ali rushed across the creaky expanse of floor followed closely by the rear guard of Di'vonte and Tyrone.

The weight of five Rangers was too much on the rain-rotted surface. Dwayne and the twins crashed through the splintering wood and soaked plaster ceiling below into the clutches of the waiting zombie hoard. Tyrone landed painfully astride a surviving floor joist. Di'vonte hung on another, his lower body dangling into the room below as he struggled to hold onto the joist and his pistol.

The building rang with death screams of doomed Rangers, as vengeance-hungry zombies chopped, sliced, and tore obscene slippery organs from their flayed bodies, feasting on their defeat. Di'vonte fired blindly down into the mob until taller attackers pulled him, howling for Tyrone's help, into the orgy of death below.

Tyrone refused to look down into that hell the Rangers deserved, but forced himself to inch painfully along the perilous joist toward his window of salvation. Hands, belly, and legs bloody and mangled from splintered wood and rusty nails, he nearly made it when someone called his name.

"Hey, Tyrone," shouted a small figure poised in the doorway of the collapsed living room. "Guess who shoudda brung me along?" It was Little Marco, grinning as he aimed Di'vonte's pistol with both hands. "You Rangers is done. I'm runin' this hood now."

"Why you with these zombies?" Tyrone whined.

"'Cause I hid'em from you Rangers," claimed the tiny mastermind. "They's my gang now—least the smart ones what do as I say."

"Don't believe it, Marco," Tyrone pleaded. "I seen it. I know how it'll go. You'll be sorry soon enough."

"Maybe so. But in my hood, even zombies gonna fight to stay alive," crowed Little Marco, as he squeezed the trigger.

DREAM LIFE

(The Rockefeller Park Greenhouse—University Circle)

"Florem Mortem Amazonia," said the Curator, tapping the thick glass window on the safe side of the greenhouse airlock. "The rarest and most dangerous plant known to man." Allan, the young graduate student standing next to him, stepped forward trying to get a first glimpse at the legendary subject of his upcoming research.

"It looks abandoned," he said, focusing on the sparse greenery visible through the small dirty window.

"It is abandoned," the elder botanist replied. "No one has been on the other side of this door in thirty years."

"How is the specimen kept alive?"

"The overhead windows provide sunlight. We circulate filtered air, steam heat the building, and occasionally run the sprinklers. What else it survives on is uncertain."

"What about maintenance on the building?"

"We maintain the exterior meticulously. Ultra-fine ventilation filters, drainage sterilization, and shatter resistant glass, which is nothing compared to the modifications installed for your study."
The Curator pointed out the new system of alcohol spray, hot steam, and ultraviolet sterilization in the containment chamber where they stood. "These will guarantee you bring nothing out of the airlock with you."

"On my isolation suit," Allan added.

The Curator agreed, "We must allow no proliferation outside this facility."

"Is that what happened before?" Allan asked. "Thirty years ago?"

"No," the elderly gentleman assured him, after a painfully extended pause. "Containment was maintained—at tremendous cost."

The young man got nothing more from his veteran companion. Allan knew the old man participated in the last study attempt. He must have been present when things went terribly wrong. Perhaps colleagues, even friends, were among the casualties. No matter, tomorrow the records of his study would be unsealed. Allan would be the first outsider to examine them in over a quarter century.

o——o

To be chosen was a huge deal. Peer reviews, special training, and psychological testing—the works—just to get into the talent pool. To be selected you needed a qualification far beyond these. You needed to be expendable.

Allan never dreamt being an antisocial unattached orphan would be a recommendation for anything. But he liked these afflictions. Pariah status afforded him more time to devote to his studies of plant life and propagation. Plants were his preferred companions. They didn't ask for anything. They would germinate, propagate, and expire in absolute silence. Immobile, unemotional, and self-sufficient they were his ultimate role models.

Safe within the locked confines of his mole-like basement efficiency, provided by the university and spartanly furnished from tree lawn cast-offs, Allan spread everything he already knew about the Amazon Death Flower on the floor around him. The legends, the discovery, the accidental collection, the ill-fated decision to cultivate, and the periodic fatal attempts of scientists to understand what they and God had wrought—all exposed at his feet.

The most delicious improbability of all...this jewel of foreboding obscurity, this Holy Grail of verdant doom, awaited him right in Cleveland, in a secret chamber of the run-down Rockefeller Park Greenhouse. What were the chances the sole survivor of the 1897

Farnsworth expedition—self-mutilated, gangrenous, and near death—would be brought back here...with a single viable seed festering in his wounds? God bless those long dead fools at the Museum of Natural History for funding such a horrific debacle.

So much accidental carnage covered his floor. Fascinating details and drawings filled with tragically failed experiments and disastrous procedural mistakes. Yet one glaring gap of knowledge remained— the means of lethality. No strangling vines, no poisonous dripping resins, or murderous thorns had ever been found. Only the primitive antidote was well documented. The Farnsworth survivor saved himself by raw physical pain—by torture that he inflicted upon himself, over and over until he escaped the forbidden valley.

The valley remained under quarantine by the Brazilian government—as forbidden now as it had been for centuries by native taboos. Why the species did not spread outside its theoretical point of origin was unclear. Perhaps its unique evolution also limited its range. So many tantalizing unknowns waited for Allan to discover and exploit.

o——o

The sealed documents and specimens from the last study attempt were laid out in the basement of Case Western Reserve University's Botany Department. The full statute of limitations had been allowed to play out—lest the university and the Curator, as the lone survivor of that research team, should be indicted on criminal or civil charges.

Of course, all former participants signed multiple waivers indemnifying everyone involved from liability. The self-same waivers Allan also signed. Still, where unexplained sudden death intersected with an increasingly litigious society, it paid to be cautious.

Wearing protective clothing and breathing apparatus, Allan and the Curator unpacked and identified each item from the original inventory. Nothing turned up missing. The previous study team had been meticulous. Timed and dated logs of each observation and experiment along with photographs and dried specimens proceeded step-by-step through the controlled propagation from collected seeds. Then quite inexplicably, the documentation turned into illegible scribbles, ending abruptly with a single black and white photograph of an unopened flower bud.

o———o

After the examinations, Allan and the Curator changed clothes. The young man simply had to ask the obvious question, "Were you there when it happened?"

"Yes and no," the old man sighed. "We'd all been in the greenhouse. Four weeks with absolutely no indication why anyone should fear this species caused us to lower our guard. Some of us thought the whole thing was hokum—or we had the totally wrong seeds."

"Sylvia asked me to go reload the camera," he said. "I wanted to sneak a cigarette outside. It was a crisp fall day—overcast as always in Cleveland, but the sun had just broken through and the colorful trees along Liberty Boulevard were spectacular that year. When I returned it was too late."

"You didn't go back in?" Allan asked. "You didn't try to save them?"

"I was alone," the Curator explained, with a strange indecipherable look in his eyes. "Afraid to enter and succumb to whatever happened, to the others. I went for help, but by that time the alarm had sounded and the authorities were involved. Because I could not explain what happened and because no one could predict the danger, the study terminated and the door was sealed."

"How many were in there?"

"Three. Professor Burrows, Louis Adelmann, and Sylvia, of course."

"So, were you close? You and Sylvia, I mean."

"No, not...not really," he stuttered. "Louie and I both had our eyes on her. But things were complicated. She was an important member of the team, quite brilliant and independent-minded, in charge of all documentation. She took the last photograph that very morning."

"Could you see what happened to them? I mean, were they bleeding or choking or anything?"

"They appeared to be asleep," he said, lost in troubled memories.

Allan would be the only one going inside this time around. Scientific hardware advanced quite a bit since the last attempt. There would be television cameras, two-way communications, and a specially constructed armband designed to deliver painful electric shocks when activated remotely from outside the airlock. He would be watched and recorded every second. He wasn't happy about that.

o———o

Allan pressed down on the airlock latch. Surprisingly it moved. He expected rust and neglect, but the mechanism, at least on this side, had been well oiled. He pulled on the heavy door and met resistance. His isolation suit felt clumsy and confining. *It will be like gardening on Mars,* he thought.

The door opened with difficulty. There was a distinct, crackling sound and a slight whoosh of air into the greenhouse. The containment chamber he left was slightly pressurized to insure nothing blew in from the dangerous side.

"Good luck," said the Curator's voice transmitted to his helmet. Allan looked back at the old man's face watching him through the window in the opposite door. Picking up his equipment box, Allan stepped through the greenhouse door and shut it behind him—saying nothing.

Inside, everything lay covered with a thick tangle of gray dried-out tendrils crackling under his steps. It would take a week to clean out a suitable workspace. Today he intended to install the cameras. He and the Curator went over their exact placement, arranged to cover every area of the greenhouse—except for one obscure corner under the raised propagation table, which Allan cunningly excluded from view.

As he reached the central aisle and turned toward the opposite wall, Allan noticed three mounds of dried tendrils on the floor. He could see human bones and a skull tightly entwined within each gray mass. The bones seemed highly weathered for being exposed only thirty years. He reached out a gloved hand to grasp one skeletal arm. It disintegrated into a fine white powder at his touch. A delicate tarnished bracelet caught his eye amid the chalky powder. *Ah, my dear Sylvia,* Allan thought. *You're looking terribly...thin, these days.*

o——o

Alarmingly, Allan could find no living specimen of the Death Flower. The sparse greenery remaining in the greenhouse proved to be common weeds—probably brought in with the original unsteril-ized potting soil. However, the voluminous dried tendrils and other plant debris did not belong to these species. Clearly some exotic growth overwhelmed the greenhouse years before—then declined and expired. Allan began careful inspection of all the collected plant material in search of its all-important seeds.

Guided by original drawings, Allan sifted through every ounce of dried material and even the chalky bone powder, which proved to be mostly calcium. Eventually he was rewarded. He began to collect tiny sliver-shaped seeds—the promise of a deadly new generation, which he carefully miscounted and stored.

o——o

At the long delayed burial, everyone had brave words to offer over the three pitifully small piles of sterilized powder, teeth, and assorted personal effects filling the brass urns. Allan was commended for his careful efforts at collecting the remains. The Curator made a stab at eulogizing those former "friends" he left to die. "These brave explorers," he extolled, with a quiver in his voice. "Martyrs in the quest for greater human knowledge," and went on blah, blah, blahing in a similar manner for nearly half an hour.

Allan had a bad taste in his mouth and jitters in his legs all afternoon. He had crushed their stupid skulls underfoot lest precious seed had fallen through an eye socket. Now he felt penalized for that by having to attend this pointless ceremony. His cheap black suit itched and he hated wearing a tie. Standing far away from the mourning relatives at Lakeview Cemetery, he soaked up the peaceful green silence surrounding him.

o——o

Propagation did not go well. Moisture, fertilizer, sunlight yielded failure. Moisture, fertilizer, shade yielded failure. Heat/cold, buried/unburied, wet/dry produced failure, failure, and more failure! Allan stayed up long nights pouring over every record of previous studies. All had occurred after far less than thirty-year intervals. Anguished fear gnawed a raw hole in his stomach. Were any of his precious seeds still viable?

Then he found it. Simple fish oil, the putrid essence of rotting sea offal, magically awakened every seed he dipped into it. Soon he had trays of small starter plants displaying the previously documented pale-green leaves with their delicate red veins. He was elated and thankful he could now proceed.

Late one day he bent down to shuffle among some flower pots stored under the propagation table. He'd done it many times before, lulling the watchful Curator into complacency. Quickly he slid into his safe corner, removed his isolation helmet and gloves, and shoved his finger deep down his own throat.

Retching as silently as possible, he threw up the remains of his lunch and the small plastic capsule he swallowed with it. Counting the seconds before his non-appearance on the cameras would be noticed, he opened the capsule and filled it with precious uncounted seeds. Then he swallowed it again.

Was this dangerously reckless? Yes, but there was no other way to get them out. If Allan was determined to change the world, as he knew and despised it, he had to swallow some major risk. No guts—no glory.

"Allan," the Curator's voice blathered, from inside the removed helmet. "Are you alright? I can't see you. I thought I heard something troubling you."

"I'm fine," Allen lied, carefully replacing his helmet and gloves before popping up into view. "I needed to clear my throat. I'm fighting a cold."

"You didn't remove your helmet did you?"

"No! You think I'm crazy? We might have to clean it out though. I had to cough up a little inside here—sorry."

"Oh, my dear boy," the Curator said. "I can't imagine how confining that outfit must be. In my day we simply wore safety glasses, lab coats, and a dust mask."

"And look how that turned out," Allan taunted.

"Yes," the Curator mused. "Well, don't worry. We have a sterile backup. I'll have this one re-sterilized overnight. Do you need to come out early because of your cold?"

"Not necessary. Thanks anyway," Allan said. But he was so excited he could barely force himself to finish the day. In this tizzy, Allan failed to notice one plant sending out its first tentative blue-green tendril in the direction of the basin of premixed fish-oil mulch.

o——o

Allan vomited mere seconds after locking his apartment door. Dry heave after dry heave produced nothing. With little in his stomach the capsule had entered his intestines. A vivid mental picture of blue-green tendrils erupting from his every orifice momentarily gave him shivers. He ran to the medicine cabinet in his grimy bathroom to swallow the variety of laxatives he had purchased—just in case.

After disgusting hours of haunting his toilet, modified with a colander borrowed from his filthy kitchen, Allan finally passed his prize specimen. He was unable to proceed directly to planting the new arrivals in the grow room he created in his only closet. His self-inflicted toilet addiction took awhile to subside.

Hours later insistent pounding on his apartment door awoke Allan from the lavatory bondage he had endured since shortly after coming home.

"Allan, Allan, are you in there?" the Curator hollered. "You must come to the greenhouse immediately! We have buds, Allan. We have flower buds!"

"I'm coming," Allan groaned. "Give me a moment." Feeling weak from his purge, he stumbled about his littered apartment—afraid to eat or drink anything lest his bowels erupt again. Instead he washed befouled hands, splashed water on his face, stripped off soiled clothing, and replaced it before answering the door.

"How could that happen?" Allan said, letting the old man enter. "I was in there only hours ago. Nothing was remotely ready to flower when I left."

"I don't know," the Curator gushed, as excited as Allan was drained. "I stayed late to file our reports. When I took a final look at the monitors the whole area around the mulch basin had changed." Having delivered this breathless revelation, the Curator relaxed enough to take in his surroundings. "Good Lord boy, what is that deplorable odor?" he gasped. "Look at this place. You live like a wild animal."

"I don't entertain much," Allan growled. "Let's go see this damn miracle."

o———o

It was true. Every Starter plant within two feet of the basin sent out at least one tendril into the smelly mulch. Obviously, these were feeder tubes, because each plant produced a thick base of foliage and shot a stem skyward. Atop each stem sat a medium-sized bud with a tight cone of narrow petals above a fleshy ovule.

"I've got to get in there," Allan said, forgetting his hunger and lethargy.

"Shouldn't we wait for daylight?" the old man quibbled.

"I'll use the night vision goggles. I want to record the first flower opening."

"Allan, wait," the Curator said, displaying Sylvia's last photo in unsteady hands. "This is exactly the moment it happened. I wasn't gone five minutes from when she shot this flower bud, until they all died." This brought the situation into focus. Allan took a deep breath staring at the photo. What happened in those last moments? Would modern precautions prove any safer than the last study team's?

"Let's test the armband," Allan decided.

Standing in the containment chamber in full isolation-suit regalia, Allan gave the nod to the old man watching through the door's window. Instantly a sharp electric pain radiated through his arm and spread all the way up his spinal column.

"Jesus Christ!" Allan shouted involuntarily.

"Count out loud until the pain fades," the Curator's voice said in his helmet. Allan counted to twenty-four before stopping. Immediately he was shocked again.

"Cut it out, will you?" he yelled. "It fucking works already!"

"We have to know how long the effect lasts," the curator reasoned. "If you succumb, it might take multiple shocks to get you back out the door. You must be prepared for that. Of course, getting angry about it will increase adrenaline flow, probably extending your intervals. So… feel free to be abusive if you must."

"I don't suppose you'd be willing to suit up and drag me out." Allan groused.

"If your suit failed, so would mine," the Curator replied. "Then who would rescue both of us?"

Right, Allan thought to himself. *I wouldn't lift a finger to save your sorry old ass either,* and went through the door. Inside everything looked dark and sinister under the red-tinted night illumination. Fear would probably also increase adrenaline flow and Allan was feeling plenty of that. He moved larger plants to better locations. Their root systems were shallow and underdeveloped. There was no doubt the tendrils provided their nutrition, and even less that their preferred meal was rotten flesh—fish, animal, bird, insect—even human. It was probably all equally scrumptious to the Death Flower. *Plants aren't supposed to experience taste, are they?* Allan pondered. *They aren't supposed to be able to smell either, but somehow they found their way to the fish-oil.*

Arranging the largest flower for his camera, he noted the inflated look of the bladder-like ovule beneath the modest petal array. He wanted to cut one of those open to examine what was going on in there. That would have to wait, because the soft hues of dawn were already showing in the windows overhead.

"Are you ready?" Allen asked. "I want this in slow motion, so increase image speed and resolution."

"I'm at triple speed," the Curator said. "Can you make out the color yet?"

"Blue I think, with lighter colored stripes. I'm uncertain of the taxonomy. *Florem Mortem Amazonia* could be one of a kind."

The wait was maddening. As the sun rose higher in the sky, the flower cones remained tightly closed. He could be too early. Perhaps the flowers would not open up for several days. The rays of direct sunlight crept down the wall and across the floor toward Allan's workstation. He was busy examining the flower cones in the improved light. With the night goggles lowered and the red night-lights off, he could make out the true colors of the clenched petals clearly. *Purple and white,* he thought. *How appropriately mortuary in context.*

As direct sunlight reached his closely studied buds, the flowers suddenly burst open. There had been no graceful gradual unfolding. It was as if someone had sprung a trap. Allan jerked back as a faint spattering of something stuck to his plastic visor. Sharp mental images of potent acid eating through plastic and onto his face flooded his terrified imagination.

"What happened?" the Curator bellowed. "Allan, are you alright?" Allan instinctively reached a gloved hand toward his face. "Don't touch it! Scrape some off into a sterile Petri dish." For once Allan was glad to follow instructions. The fright of the sudden explosion of vapor and spray had unnerved him. He wanted to run into the triple sterilization of the containment chamber like a burning man seeking water, but the voice of the older botanist held his panic in check.

"I'm alright now," Allan panted. "Thanks. I lost it for a minute."

"I don't blame you. The release was instantaneous—like an insect tripping the hairs on a Venus Fly Trap. What do you think caused it?"

"Direct sunlight," Allan guessed. "The Death Flower is light-sensitive like all plants—only violently so."

The Curator agreed. "Do you think it will snap closed again at dark?"

"Maybe," Allan reasoned. "It could be like breathing. It blows out its own pollen in the morning and sucks back in other flowers' pollen at night. The ovule should become a seed sack after pollination, then blow out the mature seeds for distribution. What else might come out, I don't know. My whole suit is spattered with something."

"Do you feel alright?"

"Yes, the isolation suit and the breathing apparatus saved me. Those poor idiots with dust masks didn't stand a chance." There was a silence, and Allan realized his affront to the Curator. "Sorry, I didn't mean it like that."

"That's alright," the subdued voice of the old man replied. "You are correct. We were so arrogant and foolish. It's almost like we wanted to die."

o——o

They spent a monstrous three days. Allan and the Curator slept on cots in the control room and called out for food. They dissected flowers and tested propagation theories. A sample of the airborne neurotoxin was sent to the chem-lab for analysis. Even day/night transitions and tropical rains were simulated. Then they brought in the sacrificial rats.

Allan named them after the apostles because he used twelve in

141

the study. The test rats were exposed, shocked painfully awake, re-exposed, revived, martyred, and recycled as flower food. The results were fascinating. The neurotoxin emitted with each morning puff of pollen did not kill them. It induced a state of total hibernation; with body functions shut down or slowed to imperceptible levels. When the victims died, they expired of dehydration and starvation, not the toxin.

This last information was particularly hard on the Curator. Human beings can live without food for about ten days. Without water, for up to five. In the coma induced by the flowers—possibly as long as two weeks. Now the old man knew Sylvia and the others could have lingered that long, awaiting the rescue, which never came.

By the end of day three they had their answers. They knew how the Death Flower grew, pollinated, propagated, and fed itself. How it likely evolved into the sole predator-scavenger in its isolated valley, as even vultures and insects drawn to its kill or blossoms succumbed to the neurotoxin themselves and were devoured. The flowers ruled, but were trapped in their isolated valley. Comatose host species were unable to travel far enough to spread the Death Flower's seeds and the surrounding jungle canopy robbed them of direct sunlight needed for expansion. Allan used these new clues to augment the historical record and reconstruct the fate of the Farnsworth Expedition.

The ethically suspect Captain Farnsworth forced a local shaman to lead his expedition to the valley. The explorer believed it held the ruins of the lost cities of Cibola. The wily shaman took them at night, by torchlight when the flowers were closed, after tropical rains had flushed the toxin from the air. At dawn the shaman had escaped, the death flowers popped open, and Farnsworth and expedition were doomed.

By chance, Private Willis and a muleskinner named Alverez were making breakfast and collapsed into the fire. The pain of their burns revived them. Unable to more than momentarily awaken their companions—even with the most brutal prodding—they felt themselves slipping back into unconsciousness. Only by placing sharp objects in their boots, and beating each other raw with horsewhips, were they able to remain awake long enough to escape the valley. The shaman's tribe awaited them in the jungle outside. Alverez was killed by their poison darts. Willis made it back to the expedition's riverboat and was evacuated to America. Apparently the extreme exertions of his escape dispelled any residual toxin from his body.

Over a celebratory beer the Curator declared a break in their marathon investigation and told Allan to go home and relax in his "rejuvenated" apartment. Allan didn't understand this comment.

"I saw how you were living, son," the Curator scolded. "You need a maid to save you from your own squalor. I called your landlord while you were busy and sent over a cleaning crew from University Housekeeping. No need to thank me."

"No!" screamed Allan. "How dare you! They'll ruin everything!"

After racing out of the Rockefeller Greenhouse, Allan arrived to find his apartment spotless and sanitized. The plastic capsule he left on the bathroom sink was gone, and his grow room closet had been unlocked, cleaned out, and now held nothing but his freshly laundered clothes. He howled in disappointment at his ruined plans to release the Death Flower on the hated intrusive cacophony of humanity oppressing him.

o——o

As he lay on his freshly made bed trying to decide how to restart his plot, he suffered a stabbing electric pain in his arm that radiated all over his body. He heard a disembodied voice yelling, "Allan, Allan, are you all right?" and found himself on the floor of the greenhouse struggling in his isolation suit. For a moment this vision produced a strong sense of déjà vu until he found himself once again on his clean bed.

Again the stabbing pain and the voice assaulted him. "Allan, wake up! It has you. Go to the door!" Again he was flailing around in the clumsy suit made worse by heavy night vision goggles hung around his neck. Again the pain and the insistent voice he thought he should recognize. "The door, Allan, the door! Crawl if you can't stand up!" The memory of the airlock door came into his mind, and he thought he could make it out through the cracked plastic visor of his helmet.

He inched his way toward it, jolted repeatedly by the stinging pain, and confused by the translucent image of his bedroom that contended with the surroundings of the greenhouse. Finally he reached the door and pulled on the latch. Falling against the door, it opened inward, and he lay half-in and half-out of the door with a pressurized wind blowing over him.

A mirror image of himself in the suit appeared and dragged him into the containment chamber, slamming the airlock door behind them. Sprays of evil-smelling liquid drenched them both. They were buffeted by an impenetrable hot fog hissing at them from every angle. Lastly a blue light bathed them in an unearthly glow, before his mirror image opened the other door and shoved him out.

The mirror image removed Allan's helmet and placed an oxygen mask on his face. "Breathe deeply, son, you made it." After fifteen minutes of pure oxygen, the neurotoxin released its grip, and the situation became even stranger.

"Congratulations," said the Curator, removing his own helmet. "You are the second known American to survive the Death Flower.

What was it like?"

"It was just like this," Allan decided. "Just like reality. Only I can't remember how I got exposed."

"It was these night goggles," the Curator said, taking them from around Allan's neck. "When you jerked back, they swung up and cracked your visor."

"Why was I wearing night goggles?"

"Because you started observing the new flower buds at two a.m. this morning. Don't you remember?"

"But that was over three days ago," Allan said in amazement.

"It was less than eight hours ago," the Curator stated, with growing concern. "What day do you think this is?"

"Friday, maybe Saturday. I was in my bedroom, and...I was in my bedroom! How did I get here?"

"Allan, try to remember. The Death Flower may have damaged your mind. Three minutes ago, more or less, the flower bud you were studying popped open. You jerked your head back and fell to the floor. At first I thought you had tripped, but when you didn't answer, I activated your armband. It couldn't have been more than twenty seconds from the moment you were exposed until I shocked you."

"Wait," Allan remembered. "I think you yelled...What was that? Allan, are you alright?"

"Yes, I did," the Curator agreed. "I think I did. We'll check the recording."

"Holy shit," Allan exclaimed. "Then everything happening to me for the next three and a half days...took twenty seconds."

"You were only dreaming, Allan. The Death Flower must make you dream."

o———o

They wrote down everything Allan could remember of his dream research on the Death Flower. The day/night, in/out pollination cycle, seed distribution, predator/scavenger evolution, semi-coma victim status, actual cause of death, and even the Farnsworth speculations. It all seemed plausible to the Curator and created a roadmap for their future actual research. Then Allan added the kicker.

"I dreamt you sent University Housekeeping over to clean up my apartment," he laughed. The Curator's strange reaction gave Allan heart palpitations.

"How did you know that? I wanted it to be a surprise."

By the time Allan sped back to his apartment, the housekeeping crew was just finishing up. An older woman opened the door holding a jumbo garbage bag stuffed with trash. "Well, well," she huffed. "If it isn't our young genius himself.

"My closet, did you..."

"Yes child, we did. You ain't allowed to grow no stinkweed in this building."

"But my bathroom, did you clean that?"

"We started in there. What was you doin' with that nasty strainer?"

"There was a plastic capsule," Allen pleaded. "I must find it!"

"You ain't gonna, honey. We flushed it and the stinkweed seeds inside. Did you know it had poop all over it?"

Allan lay on his freshly made bed and waited to be shocked again. Next time through the cycle, he would kill the old man before he made the call to housekeeping. Maybe eco-terrorism wasn't such a great idea. More rational people used assault weapons. He decided to sleep on it. The Curator gave him two days off to recover. The way Allan felt, he could sleep through all of that—dreams or not.

o———o

Two mornings later Allan awoke late. He decided to walk to work along Liberty Boulevard. If he ignored the cars, it was a beautiful few miles from his university apartment to the greenhouse. He was in no hurry. He hadn't decided whether to try again or scrap his plan, but he took a second capsule with him—just in case.

He tried to buy his bag lunch at Kenny King's, but the restaurant was closed. There was no traffic on Euclid Avenue, which was unprecedented. He found the whole Case Western campus deserted, like it was some unknown holiday. He saw his first sleepers, two old people, lying on the sidewalk outside the VA Hospital. There was a police car nearby with its doors open. The Cleveland cops were asleep inside.

Then he saw them. The purple and white flowers growing out of the street drains. Old cities like Cleveland ran their crumbling storm and sanitary sewers together under the streets. Infestation had already started and wasn't even totally his fault. Allan had to laugh. He would have done things differently. Controlled it. Focused on select targets. But this was good—God's plan so to speak. Soon *Florem Mortem Amazonia* seeds would find their way down Doan Creek to Lake Erie, and after that—who knows?

He wandered up to the art museum lagoon, found a comfortable bench with a beautiful view of the silent pastoral scene, and waited to be exposed. He took deep breaths and caught a faint hint of minty sweetness in the air. "Oh yes," he said to himself. "Now I remember that aroma," and drifted off to his untimely death on the floor of the greenhouse, with the night vision goggles hung around his neck, staring sightlessly out through the cracked plastic visor.

o——o

The Curator viewed the recording of these last moments over and over as he doctored the records and erased incriminating data.

The authorities would be suspicious, but after they examined Allan's apartment and uncovered his dastardly plot, they would back off. It had not been easy to identify a brilliant sociopath with credentials in botany.

The accidental obviousness of the cracked visor was providential. No one would look for the tiny slits he made in the breather hose. In his weakened condition Allan lasted less than three days, which was sad, but convenient. Now the Curator could resign his position leaving the future care of the precious Amazon Death Flower to its next guardian. He had completed its periodic feeding, insuring a new generation of seed stock.

The Curator went home to his comfortable house in Cleveland Heights, ate a wonderful self-prepared meal, and sat down to finalize his own research. He found this impossible. His vision blurred and his concentration fluttered back and forth from his research to some half-forgotten feelings of longing and regret. A growing lethargy overcame him.

He expired gracefully of starvation and dehydration on the floor of the greenhouse near Professor Burrows, his friend Louie, and his beloved Sylvia. The voluminous blue-green tendrils gently found openings into their ripening flesh. Morbidly curious officials and academics jostled each other for a horrified glimpse of their mysterious fate, through the small window in the sealed greenhouse door.

TERMINAL

(Tower City—Then and Now)

"You'll never guess what I seen, Man!" said the young college-age derelict verbally invading my smoking break outside the Horseshoe Casino at Tower City. I saw no reason to doubt him. He wore 1970's retro-hippie garb (bell-bottom jeans, tie-dyed shirt, and fringed leather jacket) all ripped and filthy from head to toe. His pupils were fully dilated and his speech needy and insistent. Who the hell knows what somebody like that imagines he's seen?

But I was bored with retired life and sick of losing money at slot machines. All he wanted was a willing audience and a cigarette. I offered both. His story proved wildly improbable, but definitely a cut above crack-head babble and alcoholic mumbling. He was an educated dope fiend no doubt.

"We're acid commandos," he said, beginning his colorful yarn. "But these weren't hallucinations, Man."

o———o

My buddy, Greg and I were coasting on student loans, getting high, and trying to stay out of Vietnam. It was way past midnight. There were only two open-all-night hangouts within miles of Cleveland State University, the Royal Castle and the train station under Terminal Tower.

"Come on, I got the munchies," Greg said, and off we went on our own magical mystery tour. We walked down the middle of Euclid Avenue, because the city was dead at night. The only light came from street lamps, traffic signals, and a neon ROYAL CASTLE sign promising small greasy burgers. We called them "sliders" because of their miniscule size, but at fifteen cents each it was easy to fill up. With our bellies full we still had our curiosity to satisfy. The train station came next.

Heading west down the urban canyon of Euclid Avenue from our apartment by the Arena, we aimed for the distant needle of the Tower, aglow against the night sky. Terminal Tower occupied one quarter of the frontage on Public Square, dominating that space like some huge stone idol. The bird-like building thrust its pointed beak skyward, while massive wings containing the Higbee Co. department store and the Sheraton Cleveland Hotel spread out left and right. At its feet, taking the place of talons, the arched windows and rows of brass doors flooded the sidewalk in cold white light.

A lone cab idled at the curb in hope of snagging a fare. An empty bus passed, and a cop car slowed to give us the once over, just for being awake that late. Only one door was open, but that was all we needed. Inside it was all brass and polished marble like a central bank or some Roman temple. Rows of elevators sat empty like the vacant floors piled high above us. No security guard manned the central desk and no cleaning crew swabbed the floors. Life would only be found underground at the roots of the city. To find it we descended one of the mammoth yawning ramps to the levels below.

We didn't know why there were no stairs or why the maws of those twin ramps were large enough to accommodate teams of elephants. Why they followed great sweeping curves, or why they went down at such a steep angle, we imagined one slip would cause a dangerous avalanche of tumbling humanity.

At the bottom a maze of shuttered stores surrounded us. Little cluttered shops offered obscure merchandise and services like currency exchange and shoe repair. All were locked behind folding gates. We wove our way through them toward the cavern of the railway station followed by the echo of our own footsteps.

o———o

"Holy shit," the derelict said. "It was so huge and empty. Rows and rows of long wooden benches clustered around abandoned ticket booths and gated metal stairways leading down to the tracks. The whole damn place held only one sleepy ticket agent, a half-dozen waiting passengers, a wall of vending machines, and one arrival and departure chalked on the empty schedule."

"Nobody takes the train anymore," I said, reining in his obsessive narration long enough to offer another cigarette. "We have cars and freeways now."

"Right," he agreed with a nervous laugh. "We got airplanes, submarines, rockets, and, and...God knows what else. Yeah, we got it all now. But you know why we got it? You know why we got so damn much of it now, Man?"

"No, but I bet you do."

"You're damn right, I do! And I'm not the only one—Greg seen it too! We saw it all together...but that don't matter now. Greg didn't make it out."

"I'm sorry to hear that," I lied. "But you escaped, I presume. Probably you owe it to him to get the word out."

"Yeah, I do," he agreed sadly. "It was Greg's idea to go through the door. Otherwise, we just would've wandered around till sunrise, then crashed in the park. I would never have met the twin brothers, or drank their ooze."

"Their what?"

"Their ooze," he said. "I know you never heard of it, Man. Nobody has. But all this," he added, gesturing up toward the edifice towering above us. "Is because of the ooze." Then he cast a forlorn glance out over the acres of parked cars, the multiple bridges arching over the Cuyahoga River, and the jumbled mix of industry and entertainment cluttering its banks. "And maybe all this too."

o———o

It wasn't the empty station Greg and I came to see. It was the titanic weird-ass mural displayed there. First timers used to miss their trains while hypnotized by its crazy intensity. It pulled you in like a train wreck of church windows and comic books. It was all naked giants with Prince Valiant hairdos wrestling tools, fire, and other shit. Then there were these gangs of brawny women to each side, worshiping bizarre things like microscopes and tennis rackets. All across the top, the four horsemen of the apocalypse galloped along slinging water, sunbeams, wind, and thunderbolts in all directions.

We spent many a wasted evening trying to understand its mysterious message. It covered one entire wall of the station. Each figure stood ten or twelve feet high, painted in rainbow colors on a humungous grid of metal squares. It had to mean something. Greg called it Abstract-Capitalism, but I guessed Socialist-Realism. We settled on Andrew Carnegie meets Karl Marx in Valhalla.

o———o

"I remember that mural," I interjected, between long thoughtful puffs. "It was titled *Man Overcoming Nature*...so you stoners were both wrong. There were six horsemen for your information. The rider at the center holding the sun was supposed to symbolize the god Apollo."

"That makes sense," he murmured, with an amazed look of long-delayed comprehension. "Considering what was hidden behind it."

o———o

This time Greg and I noticed something on the mural wall we never saw before. On each side of the butt-naked heroics, tucked in next to the butch priestesses of random junk, were two small doors. Dwarfed by the muscular art above them, they were virtually invis-

152

ible until that moment when the left door stood wedged open by a pail and mop. Through this accidental opening, the faint light of overhead bulbs revealed a white-tiled corridor running down into the subterranean unknown.

"What the hell," Greg said. "We're cruising for adventure aren't we?"

"Wait," I cautioned, craning my neck around the wooden benches to see if anyone else noticed this wrinkle in time and space. "We'll need provisions."

We emptied our wallets of bills in exchange for all the coins the startled ticket taker agreed to give up. The coins bought us ten candy bars, six beef jerkys, two Cokes, and a pack of Camels from the vending wall to hold off the munchies and nicotine withdrawal until morning. There was no telling how long this expedition would last, so as veteran stoners and former boy scouts, we wanted to "be prepared."

We crossed into the forbidden zone by stepping over the pail and mop. Moving them might draw attention and closing the door might cut off our escape. It takes some balls to tempt fate and the cops while tripping your ass off. But experience taught us luck and shear coincidence always favor the hopelessly trashed, because stoners are more receptive and dependent upon them.

Beyond the door the world of large spaces squeezed into claustrophobic passages of unknown purpose. We'd visited steam tunnels and boiler rooms before, but the compartments branching off the twisting white-tiled corridor seemed more like abandoned storage rooms and empty barracks. There was a vague sense of crowded former activity that long ago moved deeper down this steep spiraling pathway.

Soon evidence of even casual housekeeping disappeared and we were surrounded by serious neglect. Unexplainable machinery rusted into useless heaps in every cross-chamber. Pungent yellow seepage dribbled from the walls, trickling into a small drainage trough running down the center of the floor. The flickering overhead bulbs of increasingly antique design became less and less frequent. We were forced to continue by the faint glow of the last bulb passed and the promise of the next still functioning far ahead. Greg improvised makeshift torches from bits of discarded wood and cloth in case we lost illumination altogether.

Strangely the more desolate and abandoned our pathway became, the clearer grew the sounds and vibration of hidden activity. There was a distant rhythmic pounding as if some gigantic pile driver was working deep below. A building static buzz hovered around us, sensed more with our hair follicles than our ears.

Once the overhead bulbs completely disappeared, and before total darkness forced us to turn back, dumb luck stepped in. We discovered dim phosphorescence coming from the trickling slime trough at our feet. It wasn't much, but we went on because it seemed more reliable than our jury-rigged torches.

o——o

"Now you're just making things up," I said, to test the druggie's resolve.

"No, Man. I swear all this shit really happened," he said. "I know it sounds crazy, but I'm not even to the good parts yet."

"Well then, cut to the chase will you? I'm not standing out here all day. I thought this was about the Terminal Tower. What has all this underground nonsense got to do with that?"

"Because it ain't really a tower at all, Man."

"Of course it's a tower," I scoffed. "Look at it!" We both stood for a moment with our necks craned back as far as they would go. From this close angle it appeared more like a Victorian moon rocket with windows. At some seven hundred and eight feet, it was the second tallest building in the world when built, and the tallest building outside New York City until 1967. Sea gulls circled its lofty heights and white clouds drifted by barely escaping puncture on its needle-like flagpole.

"Believe me," he pleaded. "It's not about the tower—it's about the shaft beneath it."

"There's a shaft? How deep is that?"

"Don't know, Man. Further down than me or Greg could see and super-duper big! Like a giant manhole for dinosaurs."

"So what's the tower for?"

"To hide the monster drilling rig of course!"

"Right," I gulped at the shear enormity of his psychosis. "Go on, then."

o——o

After stumbling along in the semi-dark, Greg and I took a break to smoke, share a candy bar, and consider our options. It seemed like we'd been walking for hours, but when your brain is totally fried time perception gets squirrely. We weren't tired because of the bogus speed laced into our bootlegged acid. We hadn't followed any of the cross passages branching off to the left and right of the main corridor, so our path back seemed easy. Just follow the glowing drainage trough uphill until the light bulbs reappeared.

The question was: should we go on? We were about to flip a coin when a strange reoccurring gurgle echoed up the dark corridor. Raw curiosity, having got us this far, took over.

The closer we came the more alive the noise sounded—like someone snoring underwater. In the dim light of the slime trough the sleeping source of this weird respiration didn't seem too large or threatening. But rather than poke at it, we decided to light Greg's torch to see what we were dealing with.

The light from our match and torch in the dim corridor momentarily blinded us. When our eyes adjusted, we found ourselves facing the strangest dude either of us had ever seen. And now awakened, he was staring back at us. He was shorter than us with a wide frogish face and large moon-like eyes. He wore a sort of stocking cap and dirty coveralls with wide clown-like boots. Our torch seemed to blind and spook him. He shielded his eyes with pudgy webbed fingers and flailed about in our direction with a large metal tool of some sort.

"Hooo uwwa?' he gurgled.

Greg, being bigger than me, moved toward him waving his torch like Igor taunting Frankenstein's monster. "Noowa fwyger, noowa fwyger!" the stranger gurgled loudly.

"Cool it," I told Greg, grabbing his arm. "You're scaring him."

"I'm scaring him?" Greg replied. "Run for it! I'll hold him off as long as I can."

"Peace Man, all we need is love, remember? Let's try talking with him."

"With what...a squirt-gun?"

It was true the stranger spewed out an amazing volume of liquid with his words. But I thought I could make out some sort of English, providing his speech required equal parts saliva and breath.

Greg lowered his torch. I got him to shield it with his hand, diverting some glare from the frogman's face. Froggy lowered his tool, but continued to wave a hand back and forth restrictively.

"Noowa fwyger, noowa fwyger bwoyz. Twaa oowz bwoyz, twaa oowz!"

I wasn't sure what his beef was with better illumination, but we weren't about to douse our torch and go back to utter blindness—even momentary. Instead, I changed the subject.

"Hey Man, I'm Steve, and this is Greg. We've got snacks!" I pulled a candy bar out of my pocket, peeled back the wrapper, and took a bite. Chewing with exaggerated gusto and making as many satisfied noises as possible, I could see Froggy's attention shift. "Here, try one," I said, handing him the remainder and pulling out another for myself. He eyed it warily, but as I bit into mine, he did likewise and seemed to like it.

o———o

"Frogmen eating candy bars?" I said. "That's your idea of a good part?"

"His name was Uoothwaarg, or something like that," Steve explained. "It's hard to get enough saliva going to pronounce it right."

"Was he human? I mean is he a frog, or just frog-like?"

"Well, he had arms and legs, wore clothes, and talked...so I'm no bigot, Man. He just looked different—ethnic, you know...like way, way ethnic."

"Okay, what ethnic group did he belong to then?"

"Uhm...Aquatic-American?"

o———o

So we had a little party. Froggy had a sweet tooth and got friendly quickly. Eventually we caught on to his lingo enough to understand his torch phobia.

"Bwaa, bwaa booo!" he said, making the universal gesture of explosion. Apparently something down there was flammable, so we got rid of our torches and adapted to the slime-light again. He encouraged us to follow him on down the corridor. When we asked where we were headed, he smiled broadly.

"Bwoyz gow sneez twaa Broodarz!"

We'd never been on a trip like that, psychedelic or otherwise. It was another world. All this time we had been traipsing down a corridor which spiraled deeper around and around some unseen core, when all we had to do was follow one of the cross tunnels inward a short distance to emerge at the shaft. Shit Man, if the railroad station above was huge, the shaft itself was enormous.

Rickety industrial railings edged a narrow ledge ringing this bottomless pit. It took all our reckless courage to grasp this railing and gaze up, and even more to look down. Not that it was easy to see in either direction. Looking above, the dim phosphorescent light faded into absolute blackness beyond maybe six or seven ledge rings, each possibly a hundred feet higher than the last. Downward, the glowing slime dripped from hundreds of tunnel openings, spread across layer after layer of slippery ledges and plummeted further and further down the vertical walls. The accumulating yellowish-green glow became so intense our eyes could not make out how deep the pit plunged, or what unimaginable work went on down there.

But we could hear it. The echoing pulse of distant pile drivers, the whine of powerful rock drills, and the relentless static buzz of whatever powered them was deafening. Added to this was the hydraulic throbbing of mammoth cables, conveyors, and pistons moving up and down the shaft ceaselessly doing God knows what.

We were led to an opening in the railing where a moving cable lifted a teardrop-shaped cage even with our level. Its door snapped open and Froggy pushed us forward. We baulked momentarily from fear. The door snapped shut again shooting the cage up to the next level and leaving us teetering on the edge.

"Stoowpeed bwoyz!" our guide shouted, dragging us back from

disaster. "Uwwaz moozt gow sneez twaa Broodarz," he said, pointing upward as we waited for the next ascending cage.

That was an amazing ride. Ledge after ledge, from cage to cage, we climbed through total blackness and then into the fitfully illumination of more antique light bulbs. The shaft became smaller and smaller, and our cages more and more rectangular, until we finally stopped. The door slid open with a familiar ding and we stepped out of a standard elevator into an oak paneled vestibule facing an ornate brass door.

"Twaa Broodarz," Froggy said, smiling broadly and ushering us inside.

o———o

"So, where were you, then?" I asked.

"Up in the Terminal Tower, Man. That little round part way up there, I think."

"You think?"

"It must be," Steve reasoned. "The room wasn't very big. It was sort of round, and we could see Cleveland out the windows. You know, from way up high."

"I've been up to the observation deck," I said. "Thousands and thousands of people have. I never saw anyplace like that."

"I don't think it's on the regular tour, Man."

"What about this damn shaft thing? You talk like the whole Tower is hollow."

"I think it's all hidden by the elevator system," he said. "I mean there're rows and rows of them, and you never get to see what's behind or between them. By the time you get all the way to the top it's just one little elevator."

"So what's up there?" I asked.

"Like I told you before," he said. "The twin Brothers and their ooze!"

o——o

The room was a wild mixture of Gilded Age opulence and science fiction gadgetry, a boardroom cum laboratory with a grand oak table surrounded by impressive chairs, marble walls lined with tall windows, and bookcases overflowing with paperwork. Encrusting these walls and climbing up the bookcases and windows were braided tentacles of machinery, tubes, and plumbing all leading to a futuristic dynamo hung from the high ceiling above the table.

Greg and I recognized this piece of whirling technology immediately, although we had no idea what it did. Its mysterious image occupied a central panel of the mural in the train station.

"What have we here?" asked a raspy voice from the far end of the table.

"Bwoyz foom ooutznyed," said Froggy, closing the door behind us.

"Outsiders?' chirped a similar voice. "Where did you find them?"

"Dwwyn twaa toounaalz, Broodarz."

Until that moment, the dynamo hovering above us seemed the strangest thing in the room. Now our attention switched to its even more bizarre occupants. Three of the chairs were filled with fatter senior versions of our guide, dressed in robber baron tuxedos. If our friend from the tunnel looked somewhat frog-ish, his older bosses were definitely toad-ly.

Stranger still were the twin human brothers in the room. At least their identical shriveled faces appeared and sounded human. Their bodies however, were wheeled collections of withered organs sustained by a confusion of tangled technology and prosthetics.

"Well, well," one brother said, wheeling around the table to inspect us. "It's been quite a while since anyone wandered in on us."

"Decades at least," the other said from a distance. "Ask them what they want."

"We don't want anything," I said. "We're only exploring."

"Exploring?" the first said. "Imagine wasting valuable time like that."

"Trespassing is more like it," the other sneered.

"Twaa bwoyz haawf fooudz," Froggy added.

"Food from outside?" the friendlier brother said. "We haven't had any in years."

"Decades!" the other shouted. "Well, what are you waiting for? Give it here!"

So we had another party. The Brothers took everything we had left and divided it up with their toad partners, who even ate our cigarettes. Greg and I got none of it. By then we were wasted big time and feeling a little sick—coming down from the acid and needing to crash. But the sugar buzz from our snacks seemed to make the Brothers positively giddy. They rattled on and on about the Vaarg, their ooze, the indians, and their whirling dynamo.

o——o

"These weren't Otis and Mantis Van Sweringen, the brothers who built the Terminal Tower were they?" I asked.

"Maybe. They acted like they owned the place," Steve answered.

"Bullshit! The Van Sweringens died in the nineteen thirties!"

"Yeah? Well, they looked kind of back from the dead-ish."

Now I was thoroughly frustrated by Steve's ridiculous delusion and the meandering way he told it. I wanted some answers. "What the hell are you talking about?" I yelled. "Who are these Vaarg, what indians, what dynamo, and what is the God-damned ooze?"

"It's compressed time," Steve explained. "All the time since the Big Bang I think. Gravity squeezed it down into this mucus-like stuff in the planet's core. But sometimes, here and there, it bubbles up. Like, have you ever heard the Terminal Tower was built on quicksand?"

"I might have heard of that," I conceded.

"That was the ooze! The Vaarg use it to power everything. They got the local Erie indians to help collect it. But the other indian tribes wiped the Erie tribe out long before white people arrived because the Erie interbred with the Vaarg, and used the ooze to make poison arrows.

"Wait, you cannot compress time."

"Why not?" Steve said. "Dead dinosaurs and plants get squeezed down into oil don't they? Even plain old coal squishes into diamonds if you wait long enough."

"All right, forget that for a moment, what about these Vaarg guys?"

"They're prehistoric amphibioids who live in lake Erie and control things behind the scenes around here."

"And the dynamo hanging from the ceiling?"

"Some guy named Tesla built it using Vaarg technology. It converts evaporating time into power, which radiates through the air without wires or anything. It runs everything in the Terminal Tower and maybe all of Cleveland."

"Prove it," I said.

"I can't," Steve admitted. "But the old Muni Power Plant hasn't operated in years—yet everything keeps going. How does that work? Look Man, everybody says *time is money* and everybody knows *money is power.* So it's common knowledge—we just confuse the meaning. The Brothers use time to create power, which makes them money. They sell it all over the industrialized world."

"So according to you, evaporated time runs the world."

"*Evaporating time*, Man—the process. *Evaporated time* is like the pollution from the stuff. It's highly toxic, building up in our atmosphere because of Earth's gravity. It creates fast currents, slow eddies, and dangerous cyclic whirlpools that effect peoples' lives. The Brothers called it *temporal turbulence*. We say *time flies* or *time stands still*. We feel we're *losing time* or *making time*. Something about time just feels all wrong now—way different from how our ancestors knew it. The more evaporated time there is, the worse things get, and it's highly flammable, so..."

"It's like a time...bomb. Okay," I sighed. "If it's so damn dangerous, why do the Vaarg use it? And why are the Brothers digging a giant hole to get it?"

"Because they're greedy bastards!" Steve said. "The Brothers built Terminal Tower to drill for ooze on a titanic scale—to tap the mother lode and grab all of it."

"Then what happens?"

"They don't even know!" Steve replied. "They just laughed and claimed whatever happens, all time will belong to them...forever."

"You also said you drank it."

"Yeah, I was getting to that," he said sadly.

o———o

After the Brothers and their toad buddies ate everything, they said it was time for our reward. Froggy got a silver tray of eight tiny shot glass sippy-cups. You sucked on them to drink. He filled them from a futuristic carafe that injected a small amount of yellow vapor into each glass. Froggy passed out one glass to each of us and everybody prepared for a toast.

"What is this stuff?" Greg asked.

"We call it Skim," the jovial brother said. "The distilled essence of ooze."

"Good for what ails you and then some," claimed his cantankerous twin.

"No thank you," Greg said. "I don't think I could keep it down." Greg gave me the stink eye, indicating I should refuse also, but I'm not one to pass up a free buzz.

"You will regret your decision in the very near future," one brother told Greg.

"Never mind," I said, to spare hurt feelings. "I'll drink for both of us." I took Greg's glass and mine.

"Lucky boy," cackled the friendly twin before he toasted. "Dying men pay millions for one precious taste of time, but you get two for free. Here's to long life and the ooze!"

I sucked down both portions. I can't say exactly what Skim tastes like, but it packs a hell of a rush. I felt it race through my body from hair follicles to toenails and vanish in one whole-body shiver. My fatigue and nausea disappeared with it.

"Now you boys must be off to start your careers," the cantankerous brother said, ringing a small silver bell.

"We don't have careers," I said. "We're college students."

"You do now," said the other brother. "From now on you work for us!" Two imposing, toothy, crocodilian guards entered and laid scaly hands on our shoulders. "You start at the bottom...of the pit, and work your way up."

Our decent took longer than the trip up to see the Brothers, as our mood and destination were much lower. We had one desperate option in my pocket and agreed to try it before hitting bottom. As we were marched around a ledge to the next descending cage, we bolted for the nearest tunnel entrance. I lit a match and flicked it toward the shaft.

The resulting explosion was not what we expected. There was no sound or destruction. A blinding wave of heat and light scorched our hair and clothes and lifted us twenty yards up the tunnel. The slime trough on the floor ignited and a momentary purple flame raced up the passage, charring the slime and plunging us into total darkness.

Sounds of mass chaos echoed from the direction of the shaft, but our guards never gave chase. We scrambled down the dark tunnel clinging to each other in fear of becoming lost and alone underground. We tried to follow our plan of returning uphill to the station, but in the total darkness far below where we first met Froggy, we became completely lost.

We rested as often as we dared. Greg was having trouble keeping up. Once we were safely away from the shaft and nobody was following, I lit another match to get our bearings. I was startled to see how bad Greg looked. As a graduate assistant, he was a few years older than me. Now he looked like my father. I asked him if I looked different. He saw no change. Not wishing to alarm him, I said no more about it.

I guess we took a wrong turn, or the burning ooze blackened the white tile, but we never found the corridor spiraling upward. Eventually we ran out of matches. By that time I was carrying Greg piggyback as he wasted away to near skeletal weight.

We guessed the ooze poisoned him, although I couldn't shake the thought of swallowing the dose of Skim that might have kept him healthy. Finally he begged me to lay him down on a soft pile of charred rags.

"I can't go on," he said. "Come back to get me when you find the way out." We both knew that wasn't likely to happen. He was dying and I might never escape.

"Whatever happens," I whispered. "We had one hell of a trip."

"Yeah Man," he groaned. "Our best ever." I stayed with him until he stopped breathing and covered him over as best I could before leaving.

Wandering through the darkness, the yellow seepage began to reappear from the walls as a small amount of illumination returned. Again and again I encountered collapsed tunnels blocked with debris. I heard distant sounds of heavy machinery, but they seemed to come from above not below.

Finally losing hope, I waited on a tunnel floor for death or recapture. I heard a loud crash and a distant section of tunnel collapsed, opening a hole filled with blinding light. Crawling toward it I could smell fresh air and recognize sky and sunlight. Peeking out of the hole, I saw the muddy Cuyahoga River.

○——○

"So that's how I got out," Steve finished. "Thanks for listening, Man. I had to tell somebody. The cops would probably just hassle me."

"No problem," I said, although it felt like I'd been there all day. I checked my watch. Half an hour had passed. Time was up to its old tricks again. "So how long ago did this happen?" I asked.

"Just last night," he said.

"Last night? You saw all that, and your buddy died of old age in one night?"

"I know it sounds crazy," he whined. "What day is this?"

"Tuesday," I said, but that didn't help. Steve couldn't remember what day he and Greg went down the tunnel. He was a wacko all right. I spared him the shock of knowing this was 2015. The old Arena on Euclid Avenue was long gone, the New York Central train station was torn out of the Tower in the eighties long before the Higbee Company turned into a casino, and his colorful mural now hung in the Western Reserve Historical Society.

I gave him some spare change, my lighter, and remaining ciga-rettes. He thanked me and wandered away. Cleveland really should do more for its homeless and drug-addicted. However, if Steve actually was a young college student who went down the rabbit hole in the early seventies, then it might all be true...because he looked like he hadn't aged a day.

CONTAGION

(Tremont—Clifton Boulevard—Little Italy—The Flats—
West 25th Street)

At one o'clock in the afternoon I was having lunch at Civilization coffee house in Tremont; drinking Brazilian coffee, eating chili, jotting a few notes for my afternoon organic chemistry presentation, and people watching. Business was brisk. It took awhile to snag the perfect seat. I favor the bench seats across from the counter, with my back against the wall, and a clear view of the doors. In this so-called gunfighter position, I didn't expect any surprises. I was wrong.

He came through the front double doors looking a little confused. In retrospect, I should have tagged him as *driven*. Medium height and slightly dumpy, he had graying hair and a moustache. He wore mostly denim, denoting working class or possibly a sixties refugee. I know all this because I glanced up at him when he came through the door. Big mistake—we made eye contact—bigger mistake! I should have glanced away, but that would appear weak. I went with the cold fish-eye instead. He mistook that for interest.

"I made up my mind," he said. "To tell somebody...today." I should have stopped him there. I didn't know him and owed him nothing. I had stuff to do. It would have been easy. But, there was something about him, something about his eyes. He wore wire rim glasses with fairly thick lenses that magnified his eyes in a disturbing way. I could have walked away, got in his face for bothering me, or lied about expecting a friend. Instead I nodded. Just a slight bob of the head, a wordless approval, and an open chair was all it took. He sat down and began.

At first, I thought he was a Tea Party wacko, but he didn't mention Obamacare or Benghazi, so it couldn't have been that.

"They've been studying it for years," he insisted. "Decades, maybe.

169

It was obvious given the failure of psychology. The answer had to be somewhere else. The whole brain science thing was only a cover."

"A cover for what?" I asked, which seemed to really throw him. Not the question mind you, but the very idea someone asked a question. Somebody was actually listening. I got the impression that he'd given this rap before—to himself—probably lots and lots of times. I could see the tape rewinding in his head.

"Brain science thing was only a cover...for them, for the scientists... the government...the CIA...I don't know. It was the next logical step. Early on, it seemed like a positive idea."

Now I knew where he was coming from...conspiracy theory nut job. They're harmless. You can let them go on and on, allowing it to wash over you. Or you can play along, ask leading or ironic questions for effect, mock them or fight with them. I knew a friend who liked to stoke their fire. He'd agree totally and then take each little piece of their argument right up into the stratosphere...watch their fat heads explode.

But I wasn't like that. I just took it as another story, like what happened at the bar last night or who's going to fix your car. Another little word dance between lost souls. Only his story was a bit different, slightly deeper, a smidgen more deranged. I can't say I understood what he was jabbering about, but it had a certain dark charm. It was wild and crazy. The guy was a real showman. A couple of times I felt like clapping.

People at surrounding tables stopped their own conversations to listen. It felt like I should shush him, but, even when he quieted himself down and went all *whispered conspiracy* on me, folks at other tables would lean in. He was that addictive.

Then he mentioned the *valence principle* and things clicked for me.

He described an invisible ocean of ideas, much like the invisible atoms and molecules floating in the air...with our receptors, our brains constantly swimming through it. One idea attracts another and then another, repelling those that do not fit. Like atoms making up molecules and molecules compounds. Yeah, I could visualize that.

"So kind of like chemistry," I said.

"Exactly," he answered. "Thought chemistry, naturally occurring, predictable... controllable."

"Controllable by whom, for what purpose?"

"God, evolution, alien transmission, random chance...who knows? They were only theorizing—experimenting with the concept. Maybe it involved some unknown mental version of DNA, and what actually was the purpose of our own physical DNA?"

"Cellular communication, reproduction, evolution?" I guessed.

"According to whom?"

"Charles Darwin?"

"Who came from?" he asked.

"England?" I said, which disappointed him. I dropped the ball. "Apes?" I corrected.

"Then where did the fruit of Darwin's brain, the idea of evolution come from?" he asked, like a district attorney leading a gullible witness.

"Ape brain ideas?"

"So Darwinian theory would predict, via mutation and eons of random sexual choice...but what if our brains are only slightly more sensitive receptors than old ape brains and not the source of thoughts, ideas, or consciousness at all? What if all possible ideas were already out there in the invisible soup, waiting for a random concept, a rare catalyst, or a mutant impulse to trigger a whole generation of new, previously unthinkable thoughts to precipitate into our minds?"

He had me now. I'm sure life went on around us like always. People not close enough to be ensnared by his revelations came and went. Coffee got served. I think a shift changed, because when he released me the cute brunette with the delicate triple arrow tattoo around her left arm was gone and another barista was on duty.

I say he *released* me, but what really happened was...he finished. I can't even remember how it ended or what the last chunk of wisdom or insanity he delivered was. I only remember how his face changed. How it relaxed into blankness, as if he had totally emptied out. How his eyes, so electric before, went out...like "click," lights out—time for beddy-bye.

I think everyone listening to him experienced the same feeling. We woke up quite suddenly with some piece of a dream. Whether it was a daydream or a nightmare nobody could be sure.

Then he got up without ever eating or drinking anything, turned without the slightest word of parting, and walked out...right into the intersection of West 11th Street and Kenilworth Avenue. A Toyota Land Cruiser hit him head-on and killed him on the spot.

Everybody mobbed the front windows when they heard the tires screech. The emergency number must have received ten or twenty cell phone calls within ten seconds. The cops and EMS arrived in less than three minutes, but it didn't matter. His brain was smeared all over the pavement like a spilled cherry Slurpee.

o———o

An explosion shook the walls of the Clifton Diner. Only KABOOM and flying glass spraying the patrons with no warning. Screams came from people crawling on the floor amid the overturned dishes, silverware, and broken glass—looking for shelter. Such things were always possible in my country. But in America, in Cleveland, I am never expecting such terrible happenings.

By the mercy of the Prophet, I was not seated near a window. Unhurt, I got up to be of assistance to the injured. Gazing through the shattered window frames, across the street to the petrol station, I saw what remained of his Mini Cooper torn open from the blast and burning with horrible intensity.

I first saw his car only a short time before. Walking from my flat to the diner for supper, it sat at the edge of the car park behind the diner, close to the sidewalk. I thought it a presentable British car, red with a white top, of the most current design. Seated inside, a young man smoked a cigarette. He studied me in the side view mirror. I smiled at him. *Perhaps I will not be that sorry fellow drinking alone again in Twist nightclub this evening* I thought.

I walked past him not wanting to appear as hopeful as I felt. He exited his car and followed me. I showed him some interest as I entered the diner and walked back to my customary booth by the kitchen. He came in with some uncertainty, but seeing me, he proceeded to my booth straight away. Unaccustomed to such good fortune, I wanted to introduce myself, exchange pleasantries, but his face was strange and distant.

Perhaps he was one of those who felt it necessary for me to know of his Jesus. Those of us who perchance do not appear local, are often engaged in this manner by spiritually minded young men and women, who are nonetheless not as keen on hearing of our beliefs.

"I need to tell you something," he said, "before I go." This confused me, because we had both only just arrived. However, he was quite a nice looking chap and I was not desiring to dine alone.

"Please proceed," I said. "Let us discuss this matter over a friendly meal." He began his story with some rapidity, preferring not to order food even at my urging. I failed to understand how his story pertained to me, yet his manner of speaking was educated and of some interest. By the time my vegetarian pasta bake arrived, I had framed some humble opinion of his subject matter.

I took it some academic concern had undertaken a clandestine studying of the true nature of thought. Their experimenting produced some hitherto unknown qualities, indicating a locus of inspiration external to individual conception. He presented all of this in a most scientific manner. This attractive fellow was possibly himself an instructor or a student of chemistry. As I have no such scientific training, I found his arguments compelling but sadly almost incomprehensible.

For me, a student of the Qur'an, it was not at all surprising the thoughts of Allah should be delivered unto men already formulated. To learn the will of Allah was to obey his will, and all things are possible only through his agreement. But, I am knowing this is not the way of thinking in Christian lands.

"The experiments were successful," he announced, "but not sufficiently controlled. Infectious concepts were produced and compromised the researchers. Containment was breached. Mutations developed and multiplied."

How or why one needed to contain such a thought was unclear to me. Perhaps he spoke of heresy. Perhaps an evil influence did this work.

This I understood. Was I not myself forced to separate from my family and homeland due to my difference of desire, my own forbidden thoughts? Sadly, I am all too well acquainted with the suffering that results from such thinking.

As he spoke, I grew aware of other patrons nearby listening to his story. I felt some jealousy at their interest. Had I not been chosen to receive his attention instead of them? Let these others find a handsome Jin of their own to venerate. He was mine alone!

"Perhaps you speak of a sort of demon," I suggested, turning attention back toward me, his most devoted listener.

"Yes, absolutely," he agreed. "A poisonous concept attaching itself to any train of thought, warping it toward self-negation and emulation of the parasitic construct."

I thought of the violence and strife dividing my own land and could see this as a disease begging some cure. Sadly the efforts of one belief to eliminate others, or even to purify itself, led only to greater and greater suffering. The young man was right. Some dangerous idea had escaped in my homeland, threatening to infect us all with spreading madness.

Ensnared in such melancholy thoughts, I failed noticing the finish of my guest's most unusual remarks. The returning of conversations at neighboring tables awakened me to his sudden silence. The life and intensity of his demeanor was gone. I feared I had insulted him with my insufficient attention.

He arose without speaking and started toward the door. I called after him, but as I failed to learn even his name, my effort seemed juvenile. I followed him outside, seeing him retreat back into his car. The waiter came and admonished me to pay for my dinner. Thus I lost sight of my hopes and returned to a cold meal and many strange ideas left behind to haunt me. The explosion ended this sad meditation.

Police and fire sirens echoed throughout the area. Everyone was running out onto the sidewalk witnessing the fiery end of my dinner guest in the inferno of his ruined car.

"It was his friend," someone said, pointing the accusing finger in my direction.

"Yes, they were arguing," said another. "The bomber stormed out and drove over to the Shell station." After police forced everyone from the street and firemen doused the flames, I found myself answering a stern policeman concerning my relationship to a dead man I had barely met.

"The station attendant saw him pump gas all over the interior of his car, then get back inside and light a cigarette," the officer said. "Why would anyone do that?"

"I am not knowing," I answered. "He talked most strangely." But in a way, I did know. The reason must reside in his story. If only I understood this strange chemistry he spoke of and could remember everything said between us.

o——o

"Excuse me, Miss," he said. "May I be talking with you, please?" I was on my way to the hospital wearing my light blue scrubs. I look pretty good in them, so I guess he had his reasons. There were so many of these foreign students living around here now. They should call this neighborhood Little Pakistan or Little Japan instead of Little Italy.

I was standing in line with everyone else at Presti's for the morning rush with the number forty-three in my hand. The sign behind the counter said they were still serving number twenty-eight. He was an earnest looking little fellow with a glint of urgency in his eyes. Yearly tuition at Case Western Reserve University was out of this world, so who knows, maybe his parents owned Calcutta. I said, "Sure, what's up?" just for laughs and let him run his game.

"A very great mistake has been made," he started. "Sickness is spreading, sickness in our minds." What I considered a clumsy come-on proved to be something else. Apparently he wanted to talk with a doctor and I filled the bill. Only he didn't seem sick, only talkative.

"Our minds are defiled," he said, which seemed more spiritual than medical. Then he mentioned, "A living evil," and I realized this must be some sort of conversion rap. I've been cornered by my share of Mormons and Jehovah's Witnesses before, but never endured an Asian cold call...unless you count the Hare Krishnas at the airport.

I glanced around for an easy way out, but they were just getting around to serving number thirty. I refuse to start my shift without my latte and pastry fix, so I stuck it out.

"I'm not really into religion," I countered.

"This is no religion, Miss. We are being infected with very bad ideas. Unnatural ideas are growing in our minds." Well, I couldn't argue with that. Bad ideas are about all I hear these days. But I don't think that was exactly what he was trying to say. He was talking about bad ideas having a life of their own. Like their own agenda, apart from the person thinking them. That was kind of scary.

I tried to identify ideas I had which weren't completely under my control. Certainly my womb and libido had a few. *How many things were on my mind that I really had no interest in?* I wondered. Probably hundreds—which was pretty disturbing.

By now my diminutive guru buddy had attracted a good deal of followers. People ahead and behind us in line seemed more interested than I was.

"So what do we do about this?" I asked. That seemed to stop him in his tracks. Had he never considered this? What the hell was he doing out here testifying to all of us—if he hadn't?

"I am not knowing," he confessed. "Perhaps you may be answering this."

Me? I thought. *You expect me to come up with a fix for this?* But that's why he talked to me. He wanted help, not a hot date! When I realized I had skin in this game, my *caregiver* persona kicked in. What he described was an invisible virus, an AIDS of the mind. Not of the thought organ, of the actual brain, but of the ideas it contained. How do you eradicate that? Is there an antibiotic for evil? I kind of thought Christianity or religion in general was the prophylactic measure against such a thing. Obviously it isn't terribly effective. It's like the "Rhythm Method" of depravity control.

"Number forty-three, number forty-three," the counter person called in exasperation as I stood transfixed with the guilty number clearly visible in my hand. I responded like a sleepwalker found standing in traffic wearing a nightie.

I got a latte and two cinnamon buns. It was not until I paid and juggled my purchases that I realized my foreign suitor had disappeared. Somehow I missed his presence and felt a lack of closure. Our encounter took longer than I imagined and I took my hasty breakfast to go.

Walking down Mayfield Road toward the hospital at University Circle, I spotted the little guy. Improbably, he was standing up on the weather-beaten railroad trestle crossing above Mayfield Road. As I watched, he ran onto the tracks in front of the RTA Redline to Windmere and was obliterated by the oncoming train.

o———o

"About time," I said, as Steve resurfaced at Sal's Restaurant on West 25th Street for the first time in more than a week. "I was about to text Lisa to go knock on your apartment door...find out if you were still alive."

"I'm alive," he said, sliding into the booth with me. "I got involved with something. I had to take some time off, get myself straightened out."

"You missed a lot of classes," I said, digging into my eggs and corned beef hash. Sal's wife came by and asked if Steve wanted his usual breakfast, but he waived her off. He didn't look good. There was a drawn sleepless pallor to his face.

"I don't know if I'm going back to class," he said.

"It's too late to drop," I warned him.

"I know. I'll take incompletes, get back into studying next semester."

"So, what's her name?" I asked, hoping he had pussy trouble and not...like a brain tumor or something.

"That's the problem," he sighed. "I never even found out." I've heard quite a few tales of woe from Steve. Unrequited love is kind of his thing. He likes to suffer, thinks it makes him deep. He's not like me. I'm aware of my limits and usually aim well below them. I'm all about easy, breezy, and brief. Steve likes to shoot for the moon.

"So is she hot?" I asked.

"She's smoking hot," he began. "I was hanging out at the Harbor Inn on the West Bank on a Wednesday night, just tasting a few exotic brews at a table by the bowling machine. She was holding court at the other end of the bar. She had a bartender and five or six guys hypnotized. They'd bought her a half-dozen pricy cocktails, but she never touched any of them."

"So, what'd she look like?"

"Tall, dark hair, vivacious, baby doll face with legs and a rack to die for. She was wearing this skimpy black dress and sky-high heels like she wandered in from some rave club downtown."

"Damn, on a Wednesday, in the Flats? What's that about?"

"I don't know. But her dress looked a bit ratty, like she'd been sleeping in it since the weekend. Still, it was cut down to here and hiked up to there, so all her merchandise was clearly on display."

"Did you get her number?"

"I never even spoke to her. The guys at the bowling machine were so loud, the music was blaring, and she was so far away I could only catch a few words of what she said."

"So far out of your league you mean. You wimped-out, Steve. What's happened to my Kamikaze playmaker? You were never afraid to crash and burn before."

"It wasn't like that. Really, all I wanted to do was hear what she was talking about. She was so into it. Lecturing these guys and gesturing like some wild Italian, drawing on napkins and explaining her drawings. Smart, obsessed, passionate...I couldn't take my eyes off her. I was glued to those eyes and lips."

"You mean you wish you were glued to those lips. So, who took her home?"

"Nobody. It was the craziest thing I ever saw. They raided the place!"

"What? Who raided the place, the cops?"

"I don't know. There were tons of cops there, but they stayed outside. These guys in full HAZMAT suits burst in through the doors and dragged her away kicking and screaming. Then they came back, grabbed the bartender and all the guys around her."

"Was it drugs?"

"It must have been. They took everyone within twenty feet of her. Then they came after me."

"Holy shit," I said. "Was it terrorism or something? What did you do?"

"A big guy in a bubble suit came right at me, until I shrugged my shoulders and made signs like I was deaf or something. That seemed to stop him, but he still took my phone. They took everybody's phones. That's why you couldn't call me. The wildest thing is you couldn't talk to them. They were all shouting orders and wearing heavy noise suppressors on their ears."

"Damn, that is one hell of a bar story, Steve."

"That's not the end," he said. "The cops ran everybody out and closed down the bar. Now it's up for sale. But on my way across the parking lot, I found this." He pulled a square of dirty paper out of his pocket and carefully unfolded it on the table between us.

It was a bar napkin filled edge to edge with fevered scrawls and diagrams. It was like he found the coded formula for a hydrogen bomb…absolutely incomprehensible but still dangerous.

Steve pointed out areas he thought he understood. The words "thought cancer" and "cognitive warfare" with a prominent question mark after it were the clearest. The next most decipherable scribble was a timetable: "exposure 5-10 minutes, incubation 3-7 days, compulsive dispersion 9th-10th day" with "termination" listed immediately afterward and underlined three times. The center section was covered with an exponential dispersion diagram, with arrows radiating in all directions, each bursting out into another explosion of dispersal.

As I looked at those fevered scrawls, I could almost hear her voice, her intensity, and her desperation to get everything out—to document her torment on this flimsy scrap of paper. This was a written scream. Then I noticed Sal's wife and the patrons at the other booths around us craning their necks to get a look at her cryptic message.

"What the hell does all this mean?" I asked.

"You got me," Steve said, with a drawn desperate expression. "I just wasn't close enough to hear her. I can't make myself quit studying this damned napkin. Now I dream about it. It's like I'm inches from her beautiful face. I'm trying to read those cherry lips. But I can't make out anything over the roaring of blood in my own brain. The incessant thump, thump, thumping of my heart just won't stop! I don't know what any of this means, but I think about it constantly. It's driving me insane."

EQUILIBRIUM

(Downtown Cleveland—Gateway District)

First, I want to assure you this is nothing personal. I simply found a niche and filled it. Something any entrepreneur should understand and appreciate. Second, there are clear benefits involved. If nothing else, it could be seen as character building—for you. This was happening anyway. I simply identified the trend, found a market, and made improvements. Nothing any of you wouldn't have done if you were me. Which you aren't, because you can't be...yet. "I'm not one of you."

"So you're not from here?" said the obtuse proletarian on the next bar stool.

"Definitely not," I replied, realizing I had probably overestimated the cognitive capacity of this particular audience. Technically that did not matter. You had to tell somebody. That was the rule. Whether or not they understood or believed you...remained their problem.

"So who do you like?"

"Like?"

"You know. Who do you follow? Who do you root for?"

"I follow everyone. Other than that, I do not get emotionally involved."

"So you're like a bookie," he rationalized, on the available information he imagined he'd heard.

"Let us say, I'm an agent. Either way, there is money involved." Quite a bit actually and prestige, political influence, real estate, economic development, and its polar opposite. The ramifications filtered down through crime rates, tax burdens, life expectancy, and the like until finally settling out on such long-term prospects as infrastructure decay and civilization collapse. That was if you took a holistic perspective. But I do not. I keep things simple. I sleep reasonably well.

"So who should he bet on, the Browns or the Bears?" questioned his clueless wingman.

"You would be wise not to wager any more than either of you can afford to lose." Which was true and also a required financial disclosure. "The Bear's quarterback has been out for awhile. He could be rusty," I insinuated. This is allowed. Raised expectations and distractive speculation are totally fair play. "Remember how close the Browns came against the Patriots last week." This was a twofer. It reignited last week's bitter last-possible-minute disappointment and energized the hopeful expectations that would be mercilessly crushed this week. A few ambiguous happy platitudes, a bit of local rah-rah jingoism, a round of cheap domestic brews, and my work was done—at this establishment.

Mine's an exhausting business, and the pace will only quicken. I had a meeting later with the mayor on yet another stadium improvement extortion. Losing a major league team had been traumatic, but regaining one—and the irrational terror of going through that again—was a gift that just kept on giving. Then there was the silver-haired fox who wanted to *become* mayor in the worst possible way. His titanic ego and butt-load of cash promised unthinkable opportunities yet to come.

I had a call in to the police chief. The delicate balance of fear needed recalibration. Unarmed civilians were being gunned down weekly. The cops really had to dial back on that. Of course, with the "concealed carry" aficionados in the state house gearing-up for universal armament without permits or training, this disparity might soon take care of itself.

As I moved down Prospect Avenue toward the new Horseshoe Casino, I had to work on my pitch for expansion. It was already possible to gamble at every gas station, donut shop, and convenience store in the state, but high-stakes gambling was still far from geographic saturation. Even so, I considered that impressive for a blue state formerly limited to a handful of racetracks and Catholic bingo games.

On the corner of Ontario Boulevard I ran into my competition, which was always fun. Angelica remained cordial and upbeat as expected. She more or less had to be, because this was part and parcel of her mandate and righteous indignation wasn't her style. I, on the other hand, could go either way. Snarl or smile, it was all the same to my Boss—as long as it worked. Killing with kindness was actually my preferred approach and she expected that.

"Miss Esperanza," I said, with a polite nod. "You're looking particularly festive today."

"*Davo Ocajavati*," she replied, with a demure lowered gaze and slight shiver of fear or possibly excitement. "Sporting all black as usual I see. Is there no way I could persuade you to lighten up—just for the holidays?"

"I'm afraid not, my dear. Team colors and all that, you understand."

"I do indeed. Will I be seeing you at midnight on the new year as customary?"

"Absolutely, I would not miss it for...all of this," I said, with an expansive gesture, taking in the entire arena of our struggle.

"There's the difference between us, my dear Davo. I would gladly give up anything, sacrifice everything, for all the souls I serve."

"Happily, your Boss has already taken care of that," I joked. "Love the new shoes by the way, they're absolutely heavenly."

"Mr. Ocajavati," she giggled. "How is it whenever you say the word *heavenly*, it sounds so suggestive?"

"Practice, my dear, practice."

Before parting we arranged to enjoy a proper dinner date on a mutually neutral holiday. Those were not easy to find, "connotation" being so subjective these days. Christmas and Halloween are understandably out of the question. Good Friday could go either way, but Black Friday was considered one of mine. We settled on Arbor Day. Nature was considered a blank slate, open to being made or marred by all. One might see it as an earthly paradise, which she did. Or, one can consider it a happy hunting ground, which worked for me.

After my casino negotiations and the bankrupting of numerous blackjack players, I took a stroll to see how work progressed on the new interstate bridges. Three more years of snarled traffic absolutely boggled the mind. Imagine the hundreds of thousands of ruined commutes. Calculate the shear volume of vehicular suffering involved. The thought proved thoroughly delightful!

On the way back to Public Square, I had to pass the seasonally dormant Progressive Field. Last season had been a close one. The new Tribe manager was definitely on my shit list. Fortunately "Mr. Enthusiasm" and the other big money players in their lineup surrendered perfect zero-for-four performances at bat in that crucial final game, as their contracts with me required. The unhappy result was just what my Boss ordered. All those raised hopes and inflamed expectations dashed to pieces at the last possible moment. It was a veritable *erectile dysfunction* of civic pride, and so very, very Cleveland.

That's what I admired about this place, these people. No matter how brutally I ground their faces into the dust, they always got back up. They always came back for more. Perhaps I have Angelica to thank for that. In the South American hovel where she lived and died, all they had was dust. Dust to live in, dust to eat, and dust to look forward to, but somehow it sustained them. Brought them, or at least her, to grace. That's what my people, back in war-torn starving Croatia would have called a miracle—if they believed in miracles, which unfortunately I had not.

If I played my cards right, I would serve my entire...time, in relative comfort right here. Servicing the old Colavito contract was just a tiny part of it. There was the whole "New Browns" train wreck and of course the LeBron James affair. How could his epic betrayal have been any sweeter? And now he's returned, how many more futile expectations will he encourage and disappoint?

Of course others might strive to "move up" in the organization. Desire to manage the misery in the Middle East or Africa. But why go there? The squalor of it all was bad enough, but wars always ended. Pestilence, poverty, famine, and all the other heavy hitters were so tiresome and predictable. Why bother? Let Beelzebub, Moloch, and the other big boys wrangle around overseas, mucking about in the blood and guts. Cleveland is comfortable intimate misery and cozy limited despair. With sufficient work, I could mold it into another Detroit, minus the problematically victorious Tigers, Lions, and Pistons. There is no hurry. I have plenty of time—forever, really—to work on it.

Right now I have a shared champagne toast and chaste midnight kiss with Angelica to look forward too. That was enough. That was my tiny, forbidden taste of the paradise I forfeited long ago. Maybe it tasted a little like something she missed also.

It was too much something actually. All this rumination on questionable fraternization caused me to lose track of the time. I was late for a meeting with a certain geriatric dreamer who fancied himself an author. He was almost ready to sign on the dotted line for a book deal, as long as the "in blood" business didn't scare him away.

Of course it was not like I was still hauling around a knife, parchment ledger, and goose quill pen. We use a sort of reverse insulin injector now. Just a light prick on the finger, and you had enough to scribble most names. Unless you had one of those identity-obsessed hyphenated monikers on your hands. But *Craig A. Webb* was short enough. What we'll do in the future when writing itself becomes obsolete is uncertain. My Boss is probably funding development of a facial-recognition/DNA-coding sort of smart phone app for future negotiations.

The Tracks of My Fears

Often fellow writers voice some version of, "where did that come from, why write about this, or WHAT is wrong with you?" My duplicitous responses follow.

Lake Effect

My first published writing, found in the 1977 volume 1, number 1, of *Whiskey Island Quarterly*. It was an Edgewater offering hinting at experimentation with psychedelics, sexuality, and suicide. This rewrite adds occult anthropology and unholy miscegenation as an invocation of geographic contamination and iniquity.

Screamer

During college, I rented an old house in a dying ethnic neighborhood of southeast Cleveland. I was an outsider and folks were suspicious and insular. Next door, an old woman raved day and night behind locked doors and closed curtains. Sleep-deprived mere yards away, I wondered, *who was she yelling at and why?*

Obsession

The Main Cleveland Library was my temple of knowledge before the Internet age. Its holy of holies is the John G. White Collection, whose books are so rare and peculiar one may only read them under guard by suspicious librarians. Since every Lovecraft homage needs a forbidden book, where better to find a damnable volume?

Hunt and Gather

Police procedurals flood today's media. Forensic science and psychology solve every case in sixty minutes or less. Out on the streets however, the outcome is less certain. I imagined how real sleuths would cope, if the tide of psychotic carnage broke through the levees of reason, if human logic wasn't *all* that was involved?

Off Ramp

Our city, in the dead of night, is different from daytime Cleveland. They used to say we "rolled up the sidewalks." That's not true now in our entertainment districts. But out in the working lands that I inhabit—the factories, rail yards, and highways—night falls hard. Things happen, and one's grip on life itself can weaken and fray.

The Collection

Much has happened at the Cleveland Museum of Art lately—leadership resignations, sex scandals, and suicide. Stolen antiquities and budget shortfalls are all the buzz. Cost overruns on its ultra-modern makeover have necessitated the sale of masterpieces. I can't imagine that pleases everyone...especially the very old guard.

Slag

Heavy industry creates heavy pollution. Filling our river valley with over one hundred years of molten exploitation and suffering must conjure up something besides civic pride and prosperity. Maybe that's why it looks and smells so bad.

Small Business

The severed pigs' heads in the ethnic butcher stalls of the West Side Market are just the beginning. Throw in evilly tattooed youth, fetish prostitution, vampire romance, and the stench of Anthony Sowell's mass murders blamed on neighborhood sausage production—and it makes for quite a tasty witches' brew.

Mount Pleasant Rangers

Certain Cleveland neighborhoods suffer more than their share of horror. Be it crime or poverty, neglect or corruption, folks living there have seen enough. So local youth dedicating themselves to change should be a good thing—unless that change is bred from the festering horror itself.

Dream Life

The Rockefeller Park Greenhouse off MLK Boulevard has been eclipsed by the expensive grandeur of the Cleveland Botanical Gardens in University Circle. Still, this older collection is quite exotic. Lately its Century Plant came into hundred-year bloom. The immense flower necessitated partial removal of the roof and could be seen towering above the greenhouse. I wondered, *what else are they hiding in there?*

Terminal

My friend Greg and I preferred our substance abuse alfresco. Our all-night rambles took us to strange and forbidden places. One night we went down the rabbit hole via the art-deco wonders of the Terminal Tower, touring the bowels of our city.

Contagion

I spend time hanging out at Cleveland coffee houses, greasy spoons, and bars. There I pick up the local vibe and other spreading things. Years ago a convergence of Lovecraft and Castaneda leapt off their pages and into my psyche. Now I pass it on.

Equilibrium

With characters modeled on a perky weather girl and a scary Romanian who dated my daughter, I investigate why Cleveland seems cursed. Are we the "best location in the nation" or "the mistake on the lake?" At least we're not Detroit! What about the good stuff? What about the Gay Olympics and the Republican National Convention coming here? That's hopeful...I think...or is it?

About The Author

Craig A. Webb is an old, Buddhist, hippie clown. He has spent the years since retiring from highway work caring for his mother who has Alzheimer's, burying his father, cleaning up the tangled mess they left behind, and writing these tales. Some day he may write stories of all the wondrous inspirational places in his chosen city, stories full of love, hope, and redemption. Stories with happy endings his wife would be willing to read. But right now, he's not in the mood.

Time Wounds All Heels

Since some of these stories first saw light in the 1970's, time and entropy have been at play. Mother is gone and I have learned the cost of setting my tales in specific real locations. The Clifton Diner is no more, the Westside Market is now open on Sundays, and my father's coal-fired power plant on the shoreway is now obsolete and slated for demolition. The Terminal Tower itself faces renovation into sky-high condominiums and LeBron James broke the curse by delivering a championship to Cleveland. I'm not sure how the Vaarg feel about that. Maybe they like basketball.

www.ingramcontent.com/pod-product-compliance
Lightning Source LLC
Chambersburg PA
CBHW020446270626
47155CB00022B/1681